Mary thought of making a run for the front door, then remembered the phone by her bed. Keeping her eyes on the hall, she slid toward the nightstand.

There was another noise, not so soft this time. A footstep, followed by the sound of something—of someone—brushing against the wall.

Mary's heart bounced in her chest. Fear ran through her body like strong acid. With trembling fingers she lifted the receiver of the phone and brought it up to her ear. In the silence the dial tone seemed impossibly loud. Surely whoever was out in the hallway would hear it. Surely he would know what Mary was trying to do.

Don't miss any books in this thrilling new series:

FEARLESS™

Available from POCKET PULSE

FEARLESS™

HEAT

FRANCINE PASCAL

POCKET PULSE

New York   London   Toronto   Sydney   Singapore

An *Original* Publication *of* POCKET BOOKS

POCKET PULSE, published by
Pocket Books, a division of Simon & Schuster, Inc.
1230 Avenue of the Americas, New York, NY 10020

Produced by 17th Street Productions,
an Alloy Online, Inc. company
33 West 17th Street
New York, NY 10011

ISBN: 0-671-03948-2

First Pocket Pulse Paperback printing May 2000

10 9 8 7 6 5 4 3 2 1

To Sara Weiss

HEAT

a

Gaia had no problem understanding his broken-nose English.

long

way

from

a

blizzard

THE DEALER SMILED AS GAIA CAME

A Regular Franken-Nazi

close. "Hey," he said. He took the toothpick from between his yellow teeth and waved it through the snowy air. "You're out awful late, little girl."

Gaia Moore shoved her hands down inside her pockets and walked closer. "I'm not a little girl."

"Yeah, babe, whatever." The dealer replaced his toothpick, stomped his feet, and rubbed his hands together. "So what is it you want? I'm freezing out here."

"How sad." Gaia took a long look at the dealer. He was a big man, maybe six-foot three, with big hands, thick arms, an equally thick neck, and hair that had been shaved down to a gray stubble. A regular Franken-Nazi. Exactly the kind of guy Gaia loved to pick a fight with—especially after what had happened over the last couple of weeks. It was easy to see why big boy felt confident enough to be working alone at midnight. Most of the dealers Gaia ran into were wimps, but this guy looked strong enough to pick up a park bench and beat somebody with it.

The dealer scowled. "Hey, girl. You shopping or staring?" His big hands dipped into his pockets and came out with a display of his stock. Clumps of white crystal shoved in tiny bottles. Brown powder in glassine envelopes. "You want something?"

"Yeah." Gaia nodded as she looked at the drugs. "Yeah, I want something." She slowly took her hands from her pockets. "I want you to get out of my park."

The man took a moment to react. "Your park?" He shoved his wares into his coat. "What makes you think this is your park, chicky?"

Gaia jerked her thumb back along the path she had been following. "I live over there," she said. She pointed ahead. "And my favorite doughnuts are over there. I figure that makes everything in between mine."

The dealer was big, but his sense of humor was not. A single heavy black eyebrow crunched down over his squinted eyes. "If you're not making a buy, kid, get out of my face."

It was Gaia's turn to smile. "Make me."

The toothpick fell from the big man's lips. "You got some kind of brain damage? Hell, girl, I clean bigger things than you off my boots."

Gaia glanced down at the man's stained coat, then back at his face. "From the look of you, I wouldn't think you ever cleaned anything."

The dealer opened his mouth as if he was going to reply, then he stopped and shook his head. "You want to be nuts, you be nuts on your own time. I got business to do." He turned his big shoulders and started across the park toward the empty, snow-covered chess tables.

"You afraid of a girl?" Gaia called after him.

The dealer kept walking.

Gaia cupped her hands beside her mouth. "Police!" she shouted. "You better come arrest this asshole!"

The dealer froze. He spun around to face Gaia. "Shut up."

"Police!" Gaia shouted again. "You better hurry! He's wearing a black coat, and he's got a pocket full of crack!"

"Shut the hell up!" The dealer stomped back along the snowy path. "You want to be hurt? If that's what you want, I'll—"

"Police!"

For a big man, the dealer moved fast. He charged and swung a knotted fist at Gaia with enough force to drop a horse. Only Gaia wasn't standing there anymore. She stepped left, ducked under the man's arm, caught his thick wrist, and gave a hard tug.

Gaia's move pulled the dealer off balance. He staggered forward past the place where Gaia was crouching. Before he could turn, Gaia planted her hands against the man's broad back and gave a shove. The dealer tripped and fell facedown on the frozen ground.

4

The big man scrambled back to his feet. There was snow on his stubble-covered head and more caught in his shaggy unibrow. "I hope you like this snow," he said. "Because I'm gonna make you lick it all up."

He lunged at Gaia, but she dodged again. This time she rose up on the ball of one foot, carefully aimed a kick at the man's ribs—and slipped in the snow.

Ten thousand lessons had taught Gaia how to fall. They didn't help this time. Her feet went up, and Gaia went down. She landed on her butt with enough force to knock most of the air from her lungs and send a jolt of pain running up her spine.

The big man was on her in a moment. One big hand closed around Gaia's right arm and jerked her from the ground. The other hand drove into her gut.

The muscles in Gaia's stomach spasmed. What little air remained in her body hissed out between her teeth. Gaia gasped and strained to pull in a breath. The man tossed her back to the ground and gave her a kick that pounded into her shoulder.

He grunted in satisfaction. "I don't think you're going to make any more trouble for me, babe." He drew back his leg and aimed a second kick at Gaia's head.

Gaia rolled, put her hands under her chest, and flipped onto her feet. Before the man had recovered from his missed kick, Gaia spun and planted a punch

5

in the center of his stomach. She punched again, backed away, and followed up with a high kick that spun the man's head around.

Even though it was the guy who was getting hit, Gaia was the one feeling dizzy. She still couldn't breathe. She was fighting on nothing but the oxygen in her lungs, and that was running out fast.

If the drug dealer had been smaller, that kick would have been enough to send him flying. The fight would have been over in five seconds flat. Instead the big man only staggered for a moment, then lunged toward Gaia again.

Gaia dropped onto her hands and swept the big man's legs out from under him. As he was falling, she landed a fresh kick `square in the middle of his face`. Blood sprayed from his shattered nose. It arced away from the blow and laced across the snow in a dark red line.

For a moment Gaia froze. She looked at the snow with its stain of blood, and her mind went spinning back. A gunshot echoed through her memory. She saw her mother lying on the kitchen floor. . . .

The oxygen gauge in Gaia's body reached *E*. She dropped out of her memories and onto her knees. Air. She needed air.

The dealer groaned and started to get up. He fumbled at Gaia with sausage-sized fingers.

Gaia's stomach muscles relaxed, and she managed

to grab a lungful of air. She threw off the guy's hand, rolled away across the snow, and got up. She squeezed down another breath. The oxygen flowed into her muscles like cool water.

The dealer stood and faced her across the snow. "Ooh liddle bidch," he said.

Gaia had no problem understanding his broken-nose English. She pulled in enough air to answer him. "Let's get this over with. I want to get my doughnuts."

The big man came for her. He was more cautious this time. Gaia could see the way his eyes danced back and forth as he tried to anticipate her move. It didn't help.

Gaia waited until he grabbed for her, slipped away, and drove a kick into his side. Before he could turn, she drove another kick into his back. It was a kidney shot, illegal in any karate tournament. This wasn't a tournament.

The dealer made a deep grunt and fell to his knees. Gaia kicked him again. And again.

"Top," said the dealer. "Pweez top."

Gaia took a step back. "You going to get out of my park?"

The dealer nodded, sending fresh blood dripping from his nose.

"And you'll never come back."

"Neba. I swear. Neba."

Gaia nodded. "All right, then, go."

The dealer got slowly to his feet and stumbled away. Gaia stood and watched him until the big man was only a smudge in the snowy distance. Then she fell onto the nearest park bench.

For the space of sixty seconds Gaia was completely paralyzed. It was the cost of being stronger and faster during the fight—the price she paid for running her muscles at two hundred percent. She lay there on the bench, unable to move a muscle. She was glad that the park was deserted. The only thing worse than being helpless was having someone else see her when she was helpless.

She turned her head and saw the dealer's blood on the ground. Once again, images flooded her mind. Night. Snow. Blood. Her mother.

Gaia shook the images from her head. She propped herself up on her hands, took in a deep, cold breath, and tried to forget.

My mom loved snow, but she didn't like snowball fights. Or at least, she'd make you believe she didn't like snowball fights. Oh, no, she only came outside to enjoy the beauty of a winter's day. Snow on the tree branches. The way everything sparkled in the sun. All that shit.

She was a good actress, my mom. And if you believed her long enough to look away—pow! You'd catch a cold one right on the ear.

The best thing I remember about those snows was that the snow stayed white for a month at a time. Cloud white. White like things are in dreams. All clean and perfect.

I know that things can seem a lot better when you're remembering than they really were. But those snows really were great. Really.

City snow is not pretty snow. That's the truth. And that's the closest thing to a poem you're going to get out of me.

Back when I was a kid. Before
my mom . . . I mean, before my
dad . . . Let's just say before.
Before I came to New York City.
Back then I used to see real
snow.

I know, this is already
starting to sound like one of
those stupid stories your fat
uncle Pete tells about the good
old days. You know, the "when I
was a little kid it snowed all
year long and I had to walk ten
miles to school and we couldn't
afford shoes so I had to wear
bread wrappers on my feet and
it was all uphill both ways"
story.

Old people say things like
this because they're way into
this nostalgia thing. They want
to look back at the past and make
it so everybody was braver and
nicer and better than they are
now. They had it tough, but they
stuck together. They didn't get
anything but an orange for
Christmas, and they were happy.

They ate dirt six days a week,
and they liked it.

My story's not like that. For
one thing, I'm only seventeen, so
I didn't grow up with dinosaurs
or go hunting mastodons. The
other difference is, no nostalgia.

Let me tell you right now:
Nostalgia sucks.

All those old stories are
nothing but dressed-up lies. Who
wants to look back, anyway? I
mean, do you want to look back
and see how your mom died? Do you
really want to think about how
your father disappeared and never
bothered to so much as write? Do
you want to remember how you got
shuffled off from one place to
another and end up being forced
to live with two people you
barely know? No. Believe me,
thinking about the past is just
plain stupid.

That's why I'm just talking
about snow.

It snowed in the mountains.

Back then, I had a mom and a dad just like a regular girl. That part of the story seems like a fairy tale now, even to me, but it really did happen. I had a mother. I even have the pictures to prove it.

Of course, if you look at the pictures, you probably wouldn't think they were very good evidence. On one side you have my mom: always stylish, completely charming, totally beautiful. And then there's me. I'm . . . not my mother.

Even back in those days of yore, the Moore family wasn't exactly typical. First off, my dad was like a major government spy. Half the time he was off to some jungle or desert or foreign capital. I never knew which one because he could never talk about it. Then when he was home, Dad dedicated himself to my little problem. The Gaia-don't-get-scared-of-anything problem.

Which wouldn't have been such

a problem at all except my dad was afraid that I wouldn't get scared when I should. Which was completely wrong. Just because I'm fearless doesn't mean I'm stupid. I don't go jumping off cliffs. I don't get into a fight with more than two or three idiots at a time. Usually.

But Dad made me study every martial art in creation so I could stomp the crap out of the people I should have been afraid of but wasn't. By the time he was through, he had turned me into the muscle-bound freak girl I am today.

Snow. This is about snow.

In the mountains it snowed for weeks at a time. Not wimpy little flurries. Serious snow. And when it stopped, we would build snowmen and snow forts and snow anything else you could think of. My dad would even stop telling me about "the sixteen deadly pressure points on the human body" long enough to come outside and take part in snowball Armageddon.

Of course, not every snow was
perfect. I mean, it was snowing
on that night, too. The last
night.

Blood melts into the snow. You
might think it would spread out
and fade. Maybe it would even
turn some shade of pink. It
doesn't. Blood is dark against
the snow. That night, that last
night, it looked almost black.

Okay, now let's talk about
city snow. Let's talk about snow
in New York.

First off, it doesn't snow
that much here. People talk about
this place like it's the north
slope of Alaska, but we're lucky
to have two decent snows a year.
Every little flurry here is
treated like an emergency. Two
flakes get together, half the
city runs for home.

When the snow does fall, it
starts out white, just like moun-
tain snow. But give it two hours
on the ground, and it turns into

certified City Snow™, pat. pend-
ing.

City Snow is not a product of
nature. It looks like a mixture
of wet cement and motor oil. Ever
see a Coke Slurpee? That's pretty
close. Not the kind of stuff you
want someone to wad up and throw
at you.

I guess you could make a snow
fort in the park—if you worked
fast enough to get it done before
the snow turned to goo. You might
get in a few decent snowballs.
Maybe make a snowman, too.

But some jerk would probably
come along and mug it.

Just one
little line
would be
like **an**
ten **unforseen**
pounds of
Dove dark **effect**
chocolate.

ELLA DROPPED THE GLOWING STUB OF

a pastel-colored cigarette and heard it hiss into the snow at her feet. She shivered as she tightened the sable-edged hood around her face. The plush fur coat kept her arms and body warm, but it did nothing for the frigid wind that crept under her skirt.

Her Nature

There were at least a hundred decent restaurants in the city and another hundred that were passable. Ella fantasized about a plate of steaming alfredo at Tony's. Perhaps some black crab cake at Opaline. To get out of the wind, she would have settled for coffee at the nearest Chock Full o' Nuts. Instead she was stuck, shivering in the park, watching a little idiot who didn't have the brains to get in out of the cold.

"All right," she said. "Your little protégé finished her fight, and now she's eating her dessert. Do we have to stay out here and freeze all night?"

Beside her, a tall form shifted in the deep shadows of the winter trees. "We're watching. Isn't that your assignment?"

Ella glanced at the girl resting on the cold park bench. Was there some law that said Gaia couldn't go inside like a civilized person? For the ten-thousandth time, Ella wished she had never taken on this assignment. Not that she had been given any choice. "I watch Gaia every day. How long are we going to stay out here?" she asked.

"As long as we have to," said the tall man.

Loki stepped forward, and the light from a distant streetlamp cast sharp shadows across his rugged features. He stood with his hands jammed into the pockets of his black trench coat and his deep-set eyes focused on Gaia. "We wait until we know what we need to know."

Ella scowled. "But she's not doing anything," she said, allowing a note of complaint to creep into her voice. It irritated Ella that Loki would rather spend time out here just watching Gaia when they could be spending that time in a much more intimate way.

"Exactly." Loki turned his face toward Ella for a moment. In the dim light his eyes looked as dark as the winter sky. "And that's what we're here to observe."

"Nothing?"

Loki made an exasperated growl. "You've had months to study this girl," he said. "How many times have you seen her sit quietly and do nothing?"

Ella thought for a moment. "Not many," she said carefully.

"Not many? Try none. Not even after a fight like that. She's usually up and running as soon as she gets her energy back." Loki nodded toward the distant bench where Gaia sat in the falling snow. "The girl is restless. Headstrong. It's part of her nature." He pulled his hands from his pockets and ran gloved fingers along the rough bark of an ancient elm. "Gaia goes hunting for something to eat. Gaia goes looking for another fight. Gaia does not sit quietly and think."

Ella shivered again. "She just finished beating up some guy three times her size. Isn't that enough for you?"

Loki made a noise of disgust. "Did you see how she fought? She was slow. Clumsy. Her heart wasn't in the fight." He shook his head. "That fool should have been no problem, but Gaia came close to being seriously injured."

That thought made Ella smile inwardly. If only Gaia would hurry up and get herself killed. Ella was so tired of hearing Loki talk about the little blond-haired beast. If the girl got herself shot or stabbed or, even better, slowly and painfully beaten to death, Loki would be angry for a time, but he would recover. Best of all, Ella could leave her sham marriage and be with him all the time. That was sure to speed his recovery.

"Maybe she's sick," said Ella.

"If she has an illness, it's not caused by any bacterium or virus," replied Loki. "No. I have a good idea of what's gone wrong with our girl."

She's not my girl. Ella knew that Loki had something in mind. She wished he would just spit it out. It was far too cold for drama. "What is it?" she asked.

"Mary Moss."

It took Ella a moment to place the name. "The little junkie girl? Is that what you're worried about?"

Loki was slow to reply. "The relationship between Gaia and this Moss girl is certainly something that we must consider." Loki put his hands back into his coat pockets. "Moss and the other friends that Gaia has made. They're making her . . ." He paused for a moment, a frown turning down the corners of his mouth. "They're having an unforeseen effect."

Ella stared at him. Loki was hiding something. That wasn't surprising—Loki was always hiding some secret. It was part of his job. But this secret involved Gaia, and that made it Ella's business, too.

She clenched her teeth in frustration. Ella couldn't see what difference it made that Gaia had picked up a few pitiful friends, and she certainly didn't like the idea that Loki wouldn't tell her what was going on. "The Moss girl is nothing but a whining little addict, and that other kid, Fargo, is a cripple. Neither of them seems dangerous."

"They're far more dangerous than you know, my dear." He turned to Ella and took a step toward her. "Have you forgotten the goal of this project?"

The intensity of the look in Loki's eyes made Ella take a step back. "No, I—"

21

"Then you'll understand that for things to end up as they should, Gaia must not feel close to anyone," he said. "It's important that she not form any deep attachments."

"I understand." The explanation sounded reasonable enough, but Ella still had the feeling that Loki was hiding something. Something serious.

Loki nodded. "I have to admit that I underestimated this problem myself. I was looking for physical dangers to Gaia, not for this sort of difficulty."

A fresh gust of wind blew in among the trees. Ella shook from head to toe. "Now that we've seen her, couldn't we go somewhere?" Ella stretched her hand toward Loki's. "We don't get enough time together. We could go to your place in the Village and—"

"Not now," said Loki.

No matter how many times Loki rejected her, it always seemed to sting. Ella tried to look unaffected, but she could feel anger settling over her features. She could see no reason for them to stand there being cold. It wasn't as if Gaia was suddenly going to jump up and do something interesting.

Ella started to point this out, but quickly shut her mouth. Making Loki angry was definitely on the list of very unhealthy activities. She had already pushed her luck far enough.

"Maybe I can help solve this problem," Ella suggested.

Loki had already turned his attention back to Gaia. "And how will you do that?" he said without looking at her.

"I could forbid Gaia to go out to see these friends," Ella suggested.

Loki laughed. It was a sound as cold as the snow around them. "And exactly what good would that do? Do you really think Gaia would obey your order?"

Ella felt her face grow warm. She didn't like being reminded of the way Gaia refused to respect her commands. And she especially didn't like the tone of Loki's voice. He seemed amused by the whole idea.

"Maybe I could talk to the parents of the Moss girl," she said. "I could hint that Gaia might have trouble with drugs herself. They might keep Mary—"

"No," said Loki with a sharp shake of his head. "That kind of intervention would only cause Gaia to rebel further. I believe that in this case direct action may be required."

That was an answer Ella had no trouble interpreting. "Then what should I do? I could follow Moss and—"

"Leave the girl to me," Loki interrupted. "No, I have something else for you to do." He stopped abruptly and scanned Ella from head to spiked heels. "There's another of Gaia's relationships that concerns me. One that I think you may be particularly well suited to handle."

23

CRIMINALS WERE ALL BIG BABIES.
Just because it was dark, cold, and snowing, they were all off somewhere keeping their little toes warm. The whole park was deserted.

A Lot of Little Things

Gaia folded her legs beneath her, chomped half a chocolate doughnut in a single bite, and watched the snow fall.

The weather doofus on the eleven o'clock news was calling for six inches, but at the moment the snow was barely there. Big, heavy flakes drifted down slowly from a sky that was half clouds and half stars. It was more than a flurry but a long way from a blizzard.

Spots of cold moisture appeared on Gaia's face as the snow stuck and melted. Snowflakes caught in her hair and snagged on her eyelashes. Slow streams of melt water made their way down her cheeks, and damp spots even dared to appear on her sacred doughnut.

Memories of childhood snow were one thing, but Gaia quickly decided that getting hit in the face by real snowflakes wasn't particularly romantic. Instead it was cold and wet. Still, Gaia sat facing into the night until the collar of her sweater was damp and her long, pale hair was a wind-whipped mess.

She felt weird. There had to be a word for the emotion Gaia felt, but she wasn't sure what that word would be. It wasn't fear. She could be sure of that much. She didn't feel afraid. If her father was right, she *couldn't* feel afraid. Not ever. But if she couldn't be afraid, she could still feel sadness. And loneliness. And guilt. In Gaia's opinion, it wasn't a very good deal.

Except this feeling wasn't one of those familiar aches. This was an actual, honest-to-whatever good feeling. This was a lot of little things that added up to something that might almost be happiness. At least Gaia thought it was happiness. She didn't exactly have a great basis for comparison.

Gaia shoved the second half of the doughnut into her mouth, opened her eyes, and watched as the last of the stars vanished behind the advancing clouds. For what seemed like a century, Gaia had been holding all her secrets to herself. Now, for the first time since being forced to move to New York, she had friends she could share with.

They probably weren't friends her parents would have approved of, but Gaia's parents were long gone. Out of the picture. Mary Moss was a recovering coke addict with something of a wild streak. Ed Fargo had been a daredevil nutcase on a skateboard until an accident cured him of being crazy and left him in a wheelchair. They weren't perfect people.

But that was a good thing. Gaia could never have been comfortable with perfect people. No matter what they had been or what they had done, Ed and Mary were what Gaia needed. People that she could relax with. People that made her almost feel normal.

Only the night before, Gaia had gone so far as to tell Mary about what had happened to her mother. It might not sound like a big step, but for Gaia it was huge. Gaia never talked about her mother. Never. Not to anyone.

Talking to Mary had been one of the hardest things she had ever done. Gaia had spent so many years training to fight that taking out some half-stoned mugger barely took an effort. Her father had forced her to study so hard as a kid that high school was more like kindergarten. But telling someone else about her emotions, letting someone in on the things that had happened to her—that was hard.

Now that Gaia had slipped out a little of her past, she felt surprisingly good. Strange, but good. A little bit of the monster-outsider juice had been drained. A little of the pressure in her head was gone.

The world wasn't perfect, of course. Gaia was still an overmuscled freak. She was still stuck living with her foster parents, the Nivens, and particularly with Superslut Ella.

And of course there was the one least-perfect thing

in Gaia's world. The one that divided possible happiness from undeniable joy.

Sam Moon.

It was probably the best thing that Gaia didn't have Sam. She had only kissed him once. At least, she thought she had kissed him once. Only she had been half dead at the time, and there had been this major blow to her head, and it might possibly have been nothing but a hallucination. Anyway, one maybe kiss and Sam had already become this incredible obsession.

Gaia had already spent enough time thinking about Sam to learn a new language or become a piano virtuoso or develop a new theory of relativity. If she actually had him, actually had Sam Moon all to herself, she might short-circuit or blow up or rip his clothes off and—

Yeah, *obsession* was definitely the right word.

Thinking of the no-Sam situation took the edge off Gaia's good mood. He was probably spending his time with Heather. The insidious, ugly, ultimately evil Heather Gannis.

The image of Sam being somewhere with Heather was enough to finally pull Gaia out of her doughnuts-and snow-induced coma. She unfolded her cold legs and slid off the snow-crusted bench. It was very late. If Ella was still awake, she was going to have a fit when Gaia came in.

Gaia didn't care. She leaned back her head and whispered up to the gray clouds, each word emerging in a puff of steam.

"Come on," she said. "For once let's have some real snow."

SAM MOON LEANED BACK INTO THE

cab to pay the driver, careful to give a good tip. After all, it was the holiday season. People were supposed to be cheerful and generous.

Moonman

"Thanks for the ride, Mr. Haq," Sam said as he handed over the money.

The cabbie took it from him with a grin. "Thank you so much, Samuel," he said in English so exact, it could have come straight from the pronunciation guide in *Webster's*. A look of concern crossed the man's wide face. "Are you all right, Samuel? I haven't seen you at the tables as much as usual."

Oh, I'm fine. It's just that I'm having sex with one girl while I'm totally obsessed with another. Sam tried to smile. "Sure, Mr. Haq. As soon as the weather clears up, you'll see me in the park."

"Perhaps we will play a game then?"

28

Sam nodded. "Absolutely. I'll be looking for you."

"Good! Very good," said Mr. Haq. "I will be quite happy to take even more of your money." He laughed, gave Sam a final wave, and pulled away from the curb.

Sam turned and walked slowly up the steps to the concrete bulk of his dorm at NYU. The trouble with Gaia—the Gaia problem, as he had started to call it—was not exactly the kind of thing he could discuss with Mr. Haq. And it was definitely not the sort of thing he could discuss with his parents. His parents weren't big believers in problems.

There really isn't a problem, he told himself as he came to the door of the dorm. *I'm with Heather, not Gaia. I'm supposed to be happy now.*

Sam pushed open the door, stepped inside, and stomped the snow from his shoes. *I've got to stop thinking about Gaia. Gaia Moore is not a part of my life. Enough already.*

There was more life in the building than there had been the night before. When Sam had come scrambling back on Christmas night—in the futile hope that Gaia might stop by—the place had been all but empty. Since then a trickle of students had turned up every day. It was still more than a week before classes started up again, but already the dorms were nearly a third full.

Sam yawned as he tromped up the stairs to his

room. It had been a long day. He had called Heather first thing that morning to see if she wanted to get together, but she had said she wasn't feeling well. Considering how much alcohol she had downed the night before, Sam wasn't surprised. With Heather out of action and Gaia out of the picture, Sam had decided to hustle back home and spend a day with his parents. He didn't know if the few hours he had been able to spend at home were worth it, but at least it made him feel a little less guilty for running off on Christmas Day.

It was close to two in the morning, but when Sam walked out onto his floor, there was the familiar thick, sudsy odor of beer in the air and the ultrasonic thump of a subwoofer jolting through the walls. Someone down the hall was having a party. It shouldn't have been a surprise. The period between semesters was nothing if not an excuse to party. But Sam was way too tired to participate.

He fumbled into the quad and opened the door to his dorm room. Inside, he dropped his things, shrugged off his heavy coat, and staggered to his bed.

He wondered where Gaia was at that moment. Which was a stupid thing to wonder. Obviously Gaia would be asleep. Like any normal person would be at this hour. And wasn't he going to stop thinking about Gaia, anyway?

Sam took off his boots and lay back against the

pillow. The bass from the nearby party pounded up through the bed like some huge heartbeat. Despite the cold outside, the room suddenly felt stuffy and hot. Sam peeled off his shirt and lay on top of the sheets. He balled up the pillow and pushed it over his ears. He kept his eyes closed and did his best to think about absolutely nothing.

The sound of the bass beat kept pounding through the bed. *Thump. Thump. Thump.* Gaia. Gaia. Gaia.

Heather, thought Sam. *Not Gaia.*

Gaia. Gaia. Gaia.

Heather. I love Heather.

Liar. Liar. Liar. You. Love. Gaia.

Oh, shut up.

With a groan Sam got out of bed and walked over to his computer. If he couldn't sleep, he had to do something, and there was only one thing he could think of that might take his mind off the Gaia problem.

Sam had been a chess geek since grade school. Only that inner geek could save him now. He logged on to the Internet and went to the pogo.com game site. From there he logged in as Moonman and proceeded to the chess area. Sam bypassed the "blue" chess rooms. Those places were full of beginners and low-rated players. Even though he had been on the site only a few times, Sam's rating was already edging three thousand. If he was going to find a challenge, he would have to do it in the site's "red" room.

Sam yawned while the site loaded. It was funny how as soon as he got out of bed, he started to feel like he could sleep. He wasn't fooled. One quick game to clear his mind, then he would give the bed another try.

A scrolling list of chess games appeared on the screen. Even at this late hour most of the tables were already occupied with games in progress. At others a single name beside the board indicated someone waiting for a challenger. Sam passed up a couple of players with ratings under two thousand. He flipped to the bottom of the list and was happy to see the small silhouette of a waiting player who was rated at 2,950. It was a perfect number, within ten points of Sam's own rating.

Sam reached for the mouse and was about to join the game when he noticed the name of this perfectly matched player. *Gaia13*. He froze. It could be a coincidence. There had to be other girls in the world with the name Gaia who liked chess.

Sam's fingers began to literally tremble above the mouse button. He wanted to join the game. There was a chat facility that let the two players send messages to each other while playing. If it really was Gaia—his Gaia—Sam would have a chance to tell her some of the things that he had been thinking for the last few days.

He was going to press the button and go in. He was.

It's not her. It can't be her.

His finger touched the plastic of the button. All he had to do was click the button. All he had to do was . . .

The icon that represented a waiting player suddenly disappeared. *Gaia13 has left.*

Sam leaned back in his chair and closed his eyes. It wasn't her. The name players used on pogo was only a nickname. Just because some player used the name Gaia didn't mean it was Gaia Moore. It wasn't her.

Sam didn't believe that for a second.

WHOIS? QUERY RESULTS

Movie of the Week

Moore, Katia
No Records Found.

Whois? Query Results
Moore, Gaia
No Records Found.

Mary Moss frowned and gave her mouse a shove that sent it sliding across the desktop. She had tried a hundred different search engines and a dozen different queries, and she was still no closer to finding out what she wanted to know. There were a zillion people named Moore and at least ten thousand named Katia. But nowhere could Mary find that combination—the combination that was the name of Gaia's mother.

Ever since Gaia had decided to share the story of her mother's death, Mary had been obsessed with finding out more. The story had everything. There was violence. Murder. Mystery. And, of course, heartbreaking tragedy. Gaia Moore was a regular walking movie of the week. And Mary was a sucker for drama.

But of course, it was more than that. Gaia was Mary's friend. Gaia had saved Mary's ass, both physically and emotionally, on more than one occasion. Maybe this was Mary's chance to finally do something for her best friend.

Mary leaned back in her chair and ran her fingers through her ginger red hair. There had to be some way to get the information she was after. There had to be someplace she could go, someone she could ask.

If I only had a little blast of coke, I'd be able to think so, so much better. The idea of the drug was enough to make Mary shiver. A little cocaine would be like a glass of cold water after crossing a desert. Just one little line would be like ten pounds of Dove dark chocolate. It would be like . . . like . . .

It would be like setting your hair on fire and trying to put it out with gasoline.

Mary knew well enough that there was no such thing as just one little line of coke. One line of coke could turn into a thousand miles of white powder. Mary had only started fishing her life out of the toilet she had fallen into after her last tangle with drugs. The last thing she needed was to jump inside and flush.

Another idea occurred to Mary. She selected another site from the menu and waited until the search box came up.

ALTAVISTA ADVANCED QUERY FACILITY
moore AND katia

—No results. Try another query.—

ALTAVISTA ADVANCED QUERY FACILITY
moore AND death AND fire
—1 Result Found—

Mary almost typed a fresh query before she realized that she had gotten a hit. Quickly she snatched back her mouse and clicked on the link.

The page turned out to be the archives of a small upstate paper. The article was so different from the story that Gaia told, Mary thought for a second it was just a mistake. Then she realized it wasn't a mistake. It was a lie.

LOCAL WOMAN DIES IN FIRE

The west county home of Mr. and Mrs. Thomas Moore burned down in the early morning hours this Tuesday. Mr. Moore, an employee of the State Department, and his young daughter escaped the blaze, but Mrs. Moore was unable to leave the home in time. The county coroner's office indicates that Mrs. Moore died of smoke inhalation.

The article continued for half a column, but there was no mention of any guns. Mary ran her finger along the monitor glass. The article didn't agree at all with the story that Gaia had told her. Not even the stupidest coroner in the world would mistake a gunshot wound for smoke inhalation. And Gaia had never mentioned her house burning down. That meant either the paper was wrong or Gaia was lying.

Mary was willing to bet anything that Gaia had told the truth. That meant someone had created this story. Someone with enough pull to get just what they wanted planted in a local paper. Someone with enough power to convince local officials to lie.

Mary smiled. This story was getting better.

Mary's heart bounced in her chest. Fear ran through her body like strong acid.

a man-shaped shadow

THERE WAS NOTHING LIKE A

sleepless night to make morning look like the bottom of a
litter box.

**Boiled in
Beer**

Sam brushed his teeth for a
solid ten minutes and still
couldn't manage to dislodge the
fur that was growing on his
tongue. He stared at the face in the mirror and
winced. He was supposed to meet Heather in only an
hour. If he didn't manage to look a little less like a
refugee from *Night of the Living Dead*,
the Gaia Problem was going to turn into the No-
Girlfriend-At-All Problem.

Sam found he could think a little more clearly
about Gaia now that the sun was up. It was clear to
him that Gaia had moved on. Maybe she once wanted
to be with Sam. Maybe she had never given him a
passing thought. Maybe she had only kissed him because someone had massaged her brain with a
blunt object. One thing was sure—Gaia wasn't
thinking about Sam. According to the phone conversation Sam had held with Gaia's stepmother, Gaia had
a boyfriend.

Gaia hadn't even bothered to thank Sam for the
Christmas present he had bought for her. If there had
been a chance for Sam and Gaia the couple, that
chance was over.

There were absolutely zero odds that he was ever going to be with Gaia Moore.

So why do I keep obsessing about her?

He splashed cold water on his face and scrubbed it off with a slightly stale towel. It was like he was haunted by Gaia. He wondered if he could find a priest willing to do an exorcism.

At least I have Heather, he told himself. Then he gave himself a mental kick for having the thought. It wasn't like Heather was some sucky consolation prize. Heather was undeniably and totally beautiful. Half the guys at school were chasing Heather, and the other half didn't even feel worthy enough to try.

Oh, yeah, and there was sex. Only a few nights before there had been sex. It wasn't like Sam had a terrific amount of experience with sex, but sex with Heather was fun. It was good, no, *great*. Great sex. Any guy should feel lucky to have Heather. Having Heather was still the best thing in his life. His Gaia-free life.

Once he was cleaned up and dressed, Sam felt a little better. Less like a zombie and more like he was only terminally ill. He slipped on his coat, took a last dismal look into the mirror, and started out the door.

Before he could get all the way into the hall, another door down the way flew open and music spilled out. A short, wide-shouldered guy with curly brown hair and a broad grin stumbled into the hall. "Sam!" he cried in a voice loud enough to be heard in Brooklyn. "My favorite person in the world!"

Sam winced at the volume. "Hey, Brian." From the slurred, overloud voice and the unsteady walk, Sam could tell that Brian Sandford had a very low percentage of blood in his alcohol system.

The other student took a swaying step. "Man, it's good to see you."

Sam forced himself to smile. Something was badly wrong here. Brian Sandford was obviously drunk, but Sam didn't think he was drunk enough to forget one fact—Brian and Sam hated each other.

Brian was a local who had wandered over to NYU from the Village School. He seemed to have the same set of friends as Heather, though Sam knew Brian wasn't in the class of people that Heather would have considered the top rank. It had taken Sam several meetings to figure out that Brian had the flaming hots for Heather Gannis. He seemed to consider the fact that Heather was dating Sam as some kind of personal insult.

From the broad smile on his face, it seemed that Brian had finally recovered from his jealousy. "It's been a long time, huh?"

"I saw you two nights ago, Brian. At the Kellers' party, remember?"

Brian nodded enthusiastically. He stumbled down the hallway toward Sam and put a hand on the wall to steady himself. "Yeah," he said. "Good party. Too bad you left so soon." Brian's breath was so strong that it made Sam's eyes water. It was clear that Brian hadn't been leaving any parties early. He didn't smell like he had been drinking beer. He smelled like he had been *boiled* in beer.

"I'm glad you enjoyed it," Sam said. He closed the door to his room and zipped up his coat. "I'll be seeing you."

A heavy hand came down on Sam's shoulder. "Too bad about you and Heather," said Brian.

Puzzled, Sam turned and looked into Brian's flushed, smiling face. "What?"

"You know," said Brian. "How you guys are breaking up and everything."

He's drunk, Sam thought. *He's drunk, and he doesn't know what he's talking about.* "Did Heather say something to you?"

"Heather? Nah." Brian's red eyes closed for a moment, and his mouth gaped open. Sam could practically see the two sober brain cells in Brian's head scrambling to dredge up the memory. "It was the guys, man. They were saying how Heather was doing maid service."

"Maid service?"

41

"You know. Going from bed to bed."

A flash of cold ran up Sam's back, and he felt a sudden, metallic tightness in his guts. "They're lying."

Sam tried to put some kind of authority into his voice, but it wasn't enough to stop the flow of words that spilled from Brian's beer-saturated throat. "That's not what Charlie says."

The coldness in Sam's back began to spread into his legs and arms. There was a buzzing noise in his head. "Charlie."

"Charlie Salita. You know Charlie."

Sam did know Charlie. Charlie was a jock and a standard at all the parties Heather attended. "You're saying that Charlie Salita slept with Heather."

Brian's smile grew even wider. "Charlie says she's really hot," he said.

"He's lying."

Brain leaned in closer. "He's got details, man. He knows things about Heather."

"He's making it all up," Sam insisted.

"Charlie says your old girlfriend is a real bunny in the sack."

Sam Moon wasn't a violent person. He played chess, not football. He couldn't remember being in a real fight since junior high. None of that mattered.

He raised his right hand, carefully folded his

fingers, drew back his arm, and drove his fist straight into Brian Sandford's grinning face.

THE TRAIL OF BLOOD STRETCHED

Like a Family

across the frozen ground. Gaia bent and touched her finger to a bright red splash. Cold. The blood was as cold as the snow it was staining.

Gaia stood and looked ahead. The snow was falling so thickly that she could barely see twenty feet, but somewhere up there she could see shadowy movement. Gaia hurried along, jumping over one splash of blood after another.

Cold wind streamed through her tangled hair and brought goose pimples from the bare skin of her arms and throat. Gaia tried to remember why she was outside in such cold weather without a coat. Or shoes.

The blood trail led into a grove of stark, black-trunked trees. The shadowy figure was closer now, and the blood spots were closer together. Gaia moved faster. She had to catch up. She had to catch up before . . . she didn't know what. Something was going

43

to happen, something bad, and Gaia was the only one who could stop it.

A new shape loomed up out of the snow. It was a building. A house.

Gaia ran ahead for a few steps, then skidded to a stop in the ankle-deep snow. It wasn't just any house—it was her house. Not the brownstone she shared with the Nivens. Her real home. The house where she had lived with her parents. With her mother.

No sooner had the thought of her mother crossed Gaia's mind than a figure ran up the steps and into the house. Gaia had only enough time to tell it was a woman before the front door opened and closed with a bang.

"Mom?" Gaia ran toward the door. "Mom!"

Snow dusted the steps leading up to the door and was drifted against the sides of the house. There was blood here, too. Lots of blood. There was blood on the steps. On the porch. On the door.

Gaia pulled at the door, but it refused to open. "Mom!" she shouted. "Mom, let me in!" There was no answer from the house.

She began to hammer on the door. *Bang. Bang.*

Gaia smashed her fist against the door. The whole thing looked too fragile to stand, much less hold up to blows. Gaia struck out again, and the door rattled in its frame. She jumped and planted a solid kick. The bare sole of her foot clapped against the wood. Dust flew into the blood-stained snow.

Thump.

The boards held.

Gaia gritted her teeth. The door didn't look strong. But no matter how she battered at the aged boards, they wouldn't break.

"Gaia," called a voice from inside.

"Mom?" Gaia froze. "Mom, is that you?"

"Gaia." The voice was soft and familiar.

Gaia put her ear against the door. "Mom. It's me. Will you let me in?"

"Gaia!" This time the voice was a scream. And it wasn't Gaia's mother.

Gaia leaped back from the door. "Mary?"

"Gaia!" screamed the voice inside the house. "Gaia, help me!"

Gaia leaped, spun, and kicked the center of the door with all her strength. With a loud crash the door jumped in its frame. A thin crack split the center board from top to bottom. Fragments of wood rained down. Gaia kicked again. And again. Then followed up the kicks with a blow from a stiff right hand.

The crack widened.

"Hang on!" Gaia shouted into the opening. "I'm coming!"

She spun and directed another kick at the door, but before her foot could reach the wood, strength drained from her legs. The blow landed as only a weak thump. Gaia tried again, but this kick was even weaker.

She staggered and fell against the door. Her muscles were failing. This was supposed to happen after the fight, not in the middle. She couldn't collapse now, not when Mary was still in danger.

Gaia pushed herself away from the burned boards, drew in a deep breath, and pounded against the door with everything she had. Left hand. *Thump.* Right hand. *Thump.* Kick. *Thump.*

Blood began to pour out from under the door. Not a few spots of blood or drops of blood. Streams of blood. Buckets of blood.

The blows did nothing. Gaia was weak. Too weak to help Mary. Too weak to help anyone.

Gray fog closed in at the edge of her vision. Gaia was completely drained. Helpless.

"No," she whispered. "No, I have to get it open." She brought her hand down against the wood over and over.

Thump.
Thump.
Knock.
Thump.
Knock.
Knock.

Gaia's eyes flew open. She came off the bed in a

fighting crouch, jumped into the center of the room, and searched for the nearest enemy.

Only there were no enemies. No corpse of a house in the middle of the snowy woods. No locked door. There was only a bedroom with an unmade bed and several careless heaps of clothes.

Gaia stood there for a moment, her breath coming hard. A dream. It had only been a dream.

The knock at the bedroom door came again. "Gaia? Are you up?"

Gaia groaned. It was Ella's voice. "Yes," she admitted. "I'm up."

"Good. I've got breakfast ready."

Gaia frowned at her bedroom door. This seemed real, but she had to be dreaming. "What did you say?"

"Breakfast is ready."

Gaia wondered if that sentence had ever before passed between Ella's overly red lips. Domestic was not Ella's middle name. Gaia decided she would rather face another nightmare than eat breakfast with a bimbo. "No, thanks," she said.

"You're sure you won't grace this event with your presence?" Even through the door Ella's voice carried enough sarcasm to cut steel. "There's French toast."

"No, thanks, I . . ." Gaia blinked. Wait a minute. Replay that last statement. "Did you say French toast?"

"Yes, but if you don't want it—"

Gaia's stomach grumbled. "I, um. I mean, okay. I'll be down in a minute."

"How wonderful." From outside the door came the sound of Ella's high heels going down the steps.

Gaia looked down at her stomach. "Traitor," she mumbled. Eating breakfast with Ella was against all of Gaia's principles. Most days Ella was a bitch, pure and simple. She treated Gaia with all the warmth usually reserved for a social disease.

So what did it say about Gaia that she was willing to ignore those principles just for a little bread and syrup? "I really am weak," she said to the empty room. At least when it came to food.

She peeled off the oversized T-shirt she had worn to bed and slipped into a pair of worn cargo pants. As she rooted through the pile of clothes on the floor in search of a sweatshirt that had been worn less than three times, Gaia's thoughts returned to her nightmare.

Gaia was not a big believer in dreams. Somewhere among the thousand and one books that her father had force-fed to her, she had even digested Freud's book on dreams . Gaia wasn't buying it. Dreams were just little movies in your head, not predictions about the future. If you dreamed you were falling, it didn't mean you were going to fall. If you dreamed you hit the ground, it didn't mean you were about to die.

If you dreamed a friend was trapped, it didn't mean they were really in danger. And no matter what Mr. Freud said, not everything was about sex.

Gaia had been concerned about Mary—concern seemed to come from a different place than real fear. Which was probably why Mary had been in the dream. But there was no reason to worry about Mary anymore.

Skizz, the drug dealer who had been threatening Mary, had been on the receiving end of a patented Gaia Moore ass kicking. He had survived, but he was in the hospital. And when he got out, the police were waiting. There was no way Skizz could be a threat.

Gaia finally managed to locate a khaki green sweatshirt and tugged it over her head. She dragged her long hair free of the shirt and shook her head. It was just a dream. Dreams didn't mean anything.

She exited her room and made it down to the second-floor landing before the smell of cooking stirred her into hyperdrive. From there she took the steps two at a time.

Cooking was definitely rare behavior on Ella's part. When she did cook, Ella usually made obnoxious gourmet dishes with all the taste of old sneakers. Gaia only hoped that Ella's idea of French toast didn't involve bread and snails.

Gaia reached the bottom of the stairs and slowed her walk as she reached the kitchen. No reason to look too anxious.

George Niven sat at the breakfast table with the Sunday edition of *The New York Times* heaped in front of him. He looked at Gaia over the top of the national news section and smiled. "Hey. How are you doing this morning, kiddo? Going to have some breakfast with us?"

Gaia shrugged. "Guess so." She walked across the ceramic tile floor and sat down across the table from George.

Gaia liked George Niven well enough. George had worked with her father at the CIA for years. He had only one serious flaw. For some reason unknown to science, George was in love with Ella. And in Gaia's opinion, that was a pretty big flaw. It made her wonder just how good an agent George could really be when he couldn't even tell that the woman he had married was the world's biggest slut.

Ella marched across the room, her heels snapping on the tiles like rifle shots. Even though it was barely eight in the morning, her scarlet hair was swept up over her head, her makeup was there in all its Technicolor glory, and she was decked out in a teal dress so short, it barely qualified as a blouse.

"Here," said Ella. She inverted a pan, and two

slices of browned toast fell onto a plate. Gaia grabbed for the syrup and doused the toast in a maple-flavored flood. She was a little cautious on the first bite, but the food was actually good. Wonders would never cease.

"So," said George. "You have any plans for New Year's?"

Gaia shrugged. "I'm not sure."

George folded his paper and put it on the edge of the table. "Why don't you come with us?"

Gaia paused with a forkful of French toast halfway to her mouth. "Come where?"

"With Ella and me," said George. "I have an invitation to a New Year's Eve event down in Washington, D.C. It would be great if we all went together."

"All together," Gaia repeated.

George smiled. "Like a family."

A shiver went through Gaia, and the syrup in her mouth seemed to turn sour. Gaia barely held down her breakfast. "Uh, I . . ."

She was saved from answering by the ringing of the phone in the kitchen. A moment later Ella called from the other room, "Gaia, it's for you."

Gaia jumped up from her chair, ran into the kitchen, and took the phone from a scowling Ella. "Hello?"

"Hey," said Mary's voice at the other end. "I dare you to meet me in the park."

"I told you I'm done with truth or dare," Gaia said, smiling. "But you don't have to dare me to do that. You have something planned?"

"I'm going on an errand," said Mary. "And then to do some shopping. Come along and help me pick out something outrageous."

Gaia wasn't exactly the queen of shopping. In fact, she wasn't the princess or the duchess or the lady-in-waiting of shopping. Gaia was a shopping peasant. The trouble with shopping was that it usually involved trying things on. Trying things on usually meant looking at yourself in a mirror. Looking in a mirror meant facing the fact that your legs were as big as tree trunks and your shoulders looked like they were ready for the NFL.

"How about I skip the shops and meet you after?" Gaia suggested.

"Okay," said Mary. "Just as long as you don't try to get out of our plans for tonight."

Gaia winced. Tonight. She had almost forgotten. "Not the dancing."

"Absolutely the dancing," Mary said. "You promised."

"That's what you say. I don't remember any of it."

"You said you would go."

"I was talking in my sleep."

"It still counts," said Mary. "I better get moving if I'm going to find the perfect thing to wear tonight."

"Mary, why don't we try something else tonight? I mean, dancing, that's just not—"

"Hey, do you hear something?"

Gaia frowned. "What?"

"On the phone," said Mary. "I thought I heard something."

"Like what?"

"I'm not sure. Weird." Mary sighed. "Anyway, see you in the park around three?"

"Sure," said Gaia. Meeting in the park would give her at least one more chance to talk Mary out of her plans for the evening.

Gaia hung up the phone and went back to her breakfast. She managed two forkfuls of syrup-soaked toast before George returned to his earlier question.

"So, what about it?" he asked. "A family outing?"

"Uh, that was my friend Mary on the phone," Gaia said quickly, suddenly seeing her way out of the worst New Year's Eve on the planet with George and Ella. "I forgot I already promised to do something with her."

George frowned, but he nodded. "All right," he said. "But I'll keep the offer open. We need to do something to make this family gel."

Gaia dropped her fork and stood up from the table. A family? With Ella? One thing was sure, that was never going to happen. There might be some paper in an office across town that listed Ella as Gaia's foster mother. But paper was as much of a relationship as they would ever have.

The only thing that made Gaia feel a little better was the expression on Ella's face. From the way her forehead was wrinkled and her lips drawn down in disgust, it was clear that Ella liked the idea of Gaia as her daughter just about as much as Gaia wanted this red-haired bimbo as a mother.

THE NEW YORK PUBLIC LIBRARY

The Bat Cave

wasn't exactly Mary's favorite place. The building was a little too official. A little too *People's Court*. The last time she had been here was on a field trip back in fourth grade. Or maybe it was third. Whenever it was, all Mary really remembered was the lions.

She stopped to pet one of the stone beasts on its cold marble nose and looked up at the huge building. "Wish me luck, Leo. I'm going in."

Mary hurried up the long staircase with a cold wind blowing at her back. Inside, the library was nearly as cavernous as a football stadium. The place wasn't quite as ominous as she had expected or re-membered. Inside there were colorful displays, banks of computer monitors, and lots and lots of people.

She wandered through the stacks until she found an information desk. After getting directions, she spi-raled down a winding marble staircase, walked past an acre of book stacks, then continued downward to a smaller staircase of black wrought iron. It seemed to Mary that the stairs went down a long way. Much longer than they should have. They twisted on and on, past doors marked Archives and Records and Acquisitions, until Mary was sure that she must be several floors below ground level. It seemed to her that the weight of the whole city was pressing down on her head.

Finally, around the time Mary was beginning to wonder if the next door might be marked China, the staircase ended. The hallway she now saw had none of the intricacy or character of the building above. It was just a plain gray hall, with a concrete floor and bare walls.

Mary walked ahead cautiously. The whole place smelled of damp paper and dust. The dim light left shadows along the walls.

If I see a rat, I'm going to scream.

There were no rats. Or at least, the rats stayed hidden.

Another twenty feet along the hall Mary reached a door labeled Research. She let out a relieved breath and rapped her knuckles against the door.

"Yes?" said a muffled voice from inside.

"Aunt Jen?" Mary called. "Is that you?"

There was a rattle, and the door opened just enough to admit a head with ringlets of copper hair and round, rimless glasses. "Mary!" she said excitedly. "What are you doing down here?"

Mary shrugged. "I was on my way to the center of the earth and thought I would stop in." She rolled her eyes. "I came here to see you, of course."

"That's great," her aunt replied. Her expression suddenly changed from a smile to a look of worry. "You're okay, aren't you? You're not in trouble?"

Mary sighed. It was clear that her parents had already passed along the terrible story of Mary and her drug addiction. "No, Aunt Jen, I'm not in trouble." She held up a small manila folder. "I wanted to see if my favorite aunt could help me find some information."

Relief spread over her aunt's face. "I'm your only aunt," she said, "but I guess you can come in, anyway." She swung open the door.

Mary stepped in, but as soon as she was through the door she stopped again. "Wow! It's the Bat Cave."

Jen laughed. "Just a few simple tools."

"Yeah, right." Everywhere Mary looked, there was another computer or monitor or some other piece of electronic gear. The whole place glowed. "It looks like I came to the right person."

Aunt Jen plopped into a padded office chair and waved to another. "Have a seat and tell me what's up."

Mary sat down and opened her folder. She hesitated for a moment. What Gaia had told her was a secret. She knew that Gaia would be upset if she knew Mary had told someone else. On the other hand, Mary couldn't help Gaia unless she knew what was going on. She reached into the envelope and pulled out several sheets of computer printout. "I have this friend," she said. "Something happened to her parents."

Mary watched her aunt take the papers and study them with a frown. Aunt Jen had the same hair as Mary's mother, but that was where the resemblance stopped. Aunt Jen was ten years younger and thirty pounds heavier than her mom. And when she smiled, she looked closer to twelve than thirty-two. Even if Mary had a dozen aunts, this one would still be her favorite.

"What do you think?" Mary asked after a minute of silence.

Aunt Jen shook her head. "I don't know what to think." She flipped through the papers one more time, then looked at Mary. "I'm a library scientist. I study how to organize information. I'm not a detective."

Mary leaned forward in her chair. "Yeah, but you've got access to every piece of paper in the world."

"That's not quite true."

"It's close." Mary smiled hopefully. "Can't you make a few searches? Check a few files?"

"For what?"

"Anything you can find."

Aunt Jen gave an elaborate sigh, but there was a smile on her round face. "All right," she said. "I'll see what I can do." She glanced at her watch. "But it will have to be later."

Mary grinned. "That's fine." She got out of her chair and hugged her aunt. "Call me as soon as you find anything."

Aunt Jen led her back to the door. "You stay out of trouble."

Mary nodded. "Don't worry. I'll be fine." She turned and headed back down the gloomy hallway. Once again she felt that terrible sense of being buried under tons of earth.

I'll be fine if I don't have to come back down here, she thought with a shiver. *If I worked down here, I would have to be drugged.*

LOKI WAITED ON THE THIRD LANDING.

He could hear the girl coming closer, her leather-soled shoes clapping against the metal stairs. She was

Unseen

three twists of the stairs below, but she was climbing steadily. This girl had young legs. She would reach him soon.

He flexed his fingers. This would be a good opportunity to prevent any further threat from Mary Moss. A quick push and she would go screaming back to the bottom of the stairs. The fall was only thirty or forty feet, but Miss Moss would not survive. Loki would see to that.

The footsteps were closer now, still rising to meet him. Loki leaned over the railing. He could just make her out—two turns down.

Gaia shouldn't have told her about Katia. True, he still might have been forced to kill the Moss girl eventually. Her friendship with Gaia, if it continued, was too much of a threat. But the knowledge Gaia had shared with Mary had completely sealed her fate.

Loki squeezed his eyes shut for a moment. No one could know the truth. It was unlikely that this girl could learn anything of importance. Unlikely, but not impossible.

Mary was one turn below now. Her head was barely a foot beneath Loki's boots.

Kill her. Stop her from asking any more questions. It was the cleanest way to solve this problem.

Mary rounded the last turn and headed up to the landing.

Loki faded back into the shadows. He moved with absolute silence, and his clothes blended with the darkness. He stood absolutely still. He didn't breathe. He didn't even blink.

Mary passed within five feet of him. She could have reached out and touched him. He could have reached out and sent her to her death. But Loki had decades of experience in being unseen. Mary went on without pausing.

Loki waited until the girl had passed, then started after her. Mary would live through the day. He had decided that he didn't have enough information to act at this point. His surveillance of Mary Moss was incomplete. She might have informed others of Gaia's story.

He would have to tighten the noose around Mary. He would find out exactly what she knew and who she had told. Once those questions were answered, Loki would see that Mary Moss met with an early and tragic end.

ED FARGO HATED SALT.

Not salt on food. As far as Ed was concerned, salt was in its own food group with an importance level that put it right below the all-powerful sugar-and-chocolate group and just above the equally

Bizzaro Heather

vital grease group. Food salt was good. Unfortunately, not every grain of salt was lucky enough to end up decorating a giant pretzel.

As soon as there was the least hint of snow, the storefronts around the Village began to apply liberal amounts of salt to the sidewalk. Not little dashes of salt. Not handfuls. *Tons of salt*. Whole bags of coarse, milky rock salt. So much of the stuff that Ed wondered if there was actually more salt than snow.

There were several reasons to hate the stuff. Most of the year, being in a wheelchair was at least quiet. Now that it was salt season, every pump of his arms crunched so loudly that he sounded like he was rolling over a bag of potato chips. There was also the cleanliness factor. The salt from the wheels got all over his hands and on his clothes. And then there was the mechanical safety factor. Ed could only imagine what all the crud was doing to the chair. Salt rusted cars, and cars were covered over with nice layers of paint and all kinds of expensive antirust coatings. Ed's chair was nothing but bare metal. He wondered if the whole thing was going to melt into a puddle of rust one day and dump him in the middle of an intersection.

Ed was so involved in staring at the salt clinging to the spokes of the wheels that he almost ran over a beautiful girl.

"Hi, Ed."

Ed looked up to see Heather Gannis standing on

the sidewalk in front of him. As usual, Heather was dressed wonderfully, with a cream-colored sweater peeking from under her jacket and a matching cap of soft wool pulled down over her mass of thick brown hair. And as always, Heather looked great.

"Heather," he said. "You, um . . . You look great." *Another brilliant, insightful observation by Ed Fargo.*

Heather gave a halfhearted smile. "Thanks." She looked past Ed for a moment. "I wish I felt better."

Ed searched for the right thing to say. Back when Heather was his girlfriend, he knew what to say. Even after he and Heather had broken up, he had his patented collection of smart-ass remarks. Now that Heather was actually being nice to him again, Ed wasn't sure how to play it.

"Well," Heather said with a disappointed tone in her voice. "I guess I'd better—"

"Wait," said Ed. He gave up looking for something clever to say and went for the simple question. "What's wrong?"

Heather shrugged and looked off into the distance. "I'm not sure."

"You feeling okay? You're not sick or anything?"

"It's not me," she said. "I was supposed to meet . . . someone . . . down here, and he didn't show up. And then I saw you and I thought . . ." She stopped again and shook her head. "I probably shouldn't talk about it."

Ed stared up into Heather's face. She was pretty. Maybe even prettier than Gaia. Of course, Heather didn't have the quirky beauty of Gaia Moore, but there was only one Gaia Moore—and that was probably a good thing for the sanity of everyone involved.

Still, there was no doubt that Heather was very pretty, and at one time Ed had been convinced he loved her. Maybe he really had loved her. He had hated her, too, for the way she had left him after the accident. He wasn't sure that either one of those feelings was completely gone.

"I better go," said Heather. She licked at her lips and fidgeted with her wool hat. "It's getting late."

Ed nodded, but as Heather started to step past him he reached out and caught her by the arm. "How about some coffee?"

Heather shook her head. "I don't know if I should."

"Come on," Ed urged. "Let's have a little latte and talk."

For a long second Heather stood with her head hanging down. Then she nodded. "All right," she said. "I guess I need to talk to someone."

Ed followed her down the street to Ozzie's. It was a place famous in Ed's memory because it was the place where Gaia and Heather had first met—the place where Gaia had doused Heather with a full cup of steaming coffee.

"What are you smiling about?" asked Heather.

Ed pushed back the memory and shook his head. "Nothing," he said. "I'm just glad you decided to come with me."

For once he seemed to find the right words. Heather smiled at his response. "I'm glad you asked me."

While Heather grabbed a spot at one of the tables, Ed went to the counter and ordered for both of them. He had no trouble remembering what Heather wanted. She hadn't been Ed's first girlfriend, but she had been his first really serious girlfriend. And his last. Ed could probably remember almost everything Heather had ever ordered on their dates.

With two steaming double lattes clutched carefully in one hand, Ed rolled over to the table where Heather was waiting. She took her drink without a word and lifted the foamy brew to her mouth. As she put down the cup, she sighed. Her eyes slipped closed for a moment. "Thanks," she said. "I needed this more than you can know."

Ed took a quick sip from his own latte. He knew that Heather had been through a lot over the last couple of weeks. In fact, Ed might be the *only* one who knew everything that had happened. For some reason, Heather had trusted him with some pretty heavy secrets. Still, it wasn't like Heather to let down her guard out in public. Heather lived at the top of the high school food pyramid with the truly popular people. It was a nasty place up there, a place where you didn't dare let people know that you were less than perfect.

"Okay, now that we're stocked on caffeine and sugar, are you ready to tell me what's up?" Ed asked.

Heather put her elbows on the edge of the table and rested her face in her hands. "I don't know if I should," she replied, her voice escaping through her slim fingers. "It's not one thing. It's a lot of things. Some of it's not even really my problem."

"If it's bothering you, then I guess it is your problem."

"Maybe." Heather nodded and gave another sigh. "Maybe I do need to talk about it."

"Then tell me." Ed looked at her with what he hoped was a confident, solid expression. Your trustworthy friend Ed. "You know you can tell me anything."

The tightness in Heather's face relaxed a notch. "I always could." Heather lowered her hands and looked around her, as if afraid someone else might hear, but the coffee shop was nearly empty. Finally she looked back at Ed. "Part of it's about Phoebe," she said softly.

"Phoebe?" Ed flushed. A wave of embarrassment washed over him that almost knocked him out of his chair.

Phoebe was Heather's older sister. If anything, Phoebe was even more beautiful than Heather, though until recently she had been a little bit heavier. Not now, though. Ed had seen Phoebe only a few days before, and she had looked fantastic.

What made Ed red with embarrassment was the memory of what he had said about Phoebe. In the middle of an intense game of truth or dare, Ed had said that he wanted to sleep with Phoebe more than any woman in the world. It had been a lie, of course, and Gaia and Mary were the only ones there to hear him. Surely neither one of them would have talked to Heather. Would they?

Ed swallowed hard and tried not to look too terribly guilty. "Is Phoebe still in town?"

Heather nodded. "Just for a couple more days, though. Then she's going back to college."

A little bit of relief edged through Ed's near panic. Heather didn't *sound* like she knew about Ed's big sex-with-Phoebe confession. "So what's wrong?" he asked.

There was a long moment of silence, then Heather shook her head. "I can't talk about it. At least, not yet." A sad half smile settled on her face again. She reached across the table and took Ed's hand. "Thanks for asking me in here," she said. "I really appreciate it."

Ed tried out another reassuring smile. Anybody else at school might not recognize this soft, vulnerable person. This couldn't be Heather Gannis. Where were the biting remarks? Where was the absolute confidence? They would think this girl was bizzaro Heather. Most of the students at the Village School probably thought Heather's family was rich and Heather was a pampered princess. Ed was one of the few who knew how hard Heather worked to keep up that illusion.

"So if you can't talk about Phoebe and she's only part of it, what's the rest?"

Heather picked up her coffee, took a long drink, then set the cup down hard on the table. "Sam."

Once Ed had seen some science show where people's brains were monitored while someone read words from a list. Different words caused activity in different parts of the brain. If someone had clamped one of those helmets on Ed, the word *Sam* would have blown out the circuits.

"You and Sam are having trouble?" Ed hoped his voice didn't show as much strain as he felt. He didn't know whether he wanted Sam and Heather to be apart or not. On the one hand, if Sam stayed with Heather that meant Sam wasn't with Gaia. But Ed wasn't completely sure that he was over Heather. All things considered, Ed decided the world would be better if Sam Moon experienced spontaneous combustion. "Sam was the one who was supposed to meet you."

Heather nodded. "Over an hour ago. We were going to have lunch and maybe see a movie. Everything seemed fine."

"Except he didn't show."

"No," said Heather. "He didn't." She looked over Ed's shoulder toward the street outside. "You don't think that he knows about . . . you know."

Ed knew. "Charlie."

Heather looked around the coffee shop again, then brought her face close to Ed's. "Do you think Sam knows?"

Ed wasn't sure what to say. Charlie had gotten Heather into bed. He had bragged about it and had even used Heather for "points" in the little sex game some of the jocks had put together. "I think it's possible," Ed said carefully. "I mean, Sam's not around the Village School, but he's not on the other side of the world. What are you going to do if he finds out?"

Heather closed her eyes and put her hands against her temples. "I don't know what to do," she said. "I mean, no matter how big a jerk Charlie was and no matter what really happened, I went with him into that bedroom. Nobody made me do that."

Ed reached out and touched his hand gently against Heather's cheek. "It's okay," he said. "Sam probably doesn't know, and even if he does, I'm sure he'll understand."

Heather covered Ed's hand with one of her own and leaned against his palm. "You think . . ." She hesitated for a moment, then ventured a tentative smile.

68

"You think you would be interested in getting something to eat?"

Ed grinned. "When have I ever turned down food?"

Heather's smile brightened. "And after that—"

"A movie," Ed finished. "Sure. I'd love to."

Heather's smile grew wider and lost some of its sad edge. "I can always count on you." Then, much to Ed's astonishment, she leaned across the table and kissed him on the cheek.

MARY MOSS HELD THE HANDLE OF

That Tone

one shopping bag with her teeth, put another between her knees, and bent down to jab her key into the lock. She managed to turn the doorknob and stumble inside before everything tumbled to the floor.

"Little help here!" she called out, but the apartment was dark and quiet. Mary dragged her stuff inside and let the door swing shut.

Actually, it was probably good that her parents weren't home. For one thing, it showed that they were beginning to trust her again—even if it was for only a few hours in the middle of the day.

Since learning of Mary's drug habit, her parents

had been smothering her with everything from video-tapes and brochures on rehab centers to books from famous users who had kicked their addictions. Even her Christmas presents had been heavily loaded with an assortment of such uplifting material.

Mary didn't feel uplifted. She was off the drugs, and it wasn't because she had gone to any trendy center or been inspired by some has-been celebrity. She had kicked cocaine on her own. Well, maybe having Gaia around had helped a little. Maybe more than a little. But the point was, Mary was off the coke. If her parents were looking for the right time to give her books about drugs, they had missed it—by years.

The other reason it was good to find the apartment empty was that now her parents wouldn't see what she had bought.

Mary hefted the bags and made her way up the stairs to her bedroom. She had just enough time to get her things together before going out to meet Gaia. If she was lucky, she might even squeeze in a call to Aunt Jen before she left, in case there was any news on the Gaia's-parents-mystery front.

She gave the shopping bags a shake. Even though most of her Christmas presents had been of the ex-druggie-book variety, there had still been some cash slipped in among the pages. Not as many bills as in previous years, but then, her parents were probably afraid that if they gave her a big wad of cash, she would shove it up her nose.

Even the reduced cash supply had been enough to add some serious punch to Mary's wardrobe. She emptied the contents of the first bag onto her bed and studied the results. There were blouses she had liberated from Classics, a retro clothing store south of the park. There were some jeans that were completely too squeezy at the moment but that Mary hoped to wear as soon as she had battled off the holiday bulge. There were three pairs of shoes and a lace camisole in a violet so deep, it was almost black.

Mary smiled down at the pile. The clothes represented four hours of dedicated shopping, but they were definitely worth it. If you knew where to shop, a little bit of cash could buy a big chunk of cool.

She reached down, picked up the camisole, and carried it across to the mirror on her dresser. She held it up and was just imagining what her mother would say if she tried to wear it sans shirt when she heard a noise from the hallway.

Mary turned. "Mom?"

There was no reply.

"Mom? Are you guys home?"

For several long seconds Mary heard nothing. Then there was a soft creaking sound—the sound of boards shifting under someone's weight.

At once Mary's throat drew tight. "Mom?" she tried again, but this time it was only a faint whisper.

Slowly she let the camisole slide from her fingers and fall into a dark puddle on the floor. Moving as quietly as she could, Mary took a step toward the door. Then another. She peered out through the opening.

There was no sound from the hallway. No creaking boards. But there was a shadow. A man-shaped shadow. Just outside the limits of her sight, someone was standing in the hallway. Even without the shadow Mary didn't have to see him to know he was there—she could *feel* him.

She thought of making a run for the front door, then remembered the phone by her bed. Keeping her eyes on the hall, she slid toward the nightstand.

There was another noise, not so soft this time. A footstep, followed by the sound of something—of someone—brushing against the wall.

Mary's heart bounced in her chest. Fear ran through her body like strong acid. With trembling fingers she lifted the receiver of the phone and brought it up to her ear. In the silence the dial tone seemed impossibly loud. Surely whoever was out in the hallway would hear it. Surely he would know what Mary was trying to do.

Another footstep from the hallway. Louder this time. Closer.

Mary brought her fingers to the dial and pressed down on the nine. The tone was so loud, it made her jump. She had to close her eyes for a second and draw a breath before moving her finger over to press the one. She raised her finger to press the button again.

There was a sudden noise from downstairs. A clatter followed by the squeak of the door being shoved open.

"Mary, honey?" called a voice from downstairs. "Are you home?"

Mary felt a wash of relief so strong, she almost fell. "Dad!" she called out. "I'm up here." But as soon as she spoke Mary realized that her parents could also be in danger. "Watch out!" she shouted. "There's someone else up here!"

Footsteps sounded from the stairs. "What did you say?" called her father.

Mary let the phone drop and jumped to her door. "Stay back, Dad! There's someone—"

But there was no one. In both directions the hallway was empty.

Her father reached the top of the stairs. "Who did you say was here?"

Mary looked along the empty hall and shook her head. "I heard . . . I mean, I thought . . ." She paused, then shrugged. "Nobody, I guess."

Her father's face turned down in an expression of concern. "Are you okay?"

73

The tone of his voice made Mary wince. It was a tone she had heard all too often lately. No matter what the words, anytime her parents asked her a question in that tone, she knew what they were really asking—was she on drugs?

"I'm fine," Mary said. "Just fine." She backed into her bedroom and closed the door.

THERE HAD TO BE A BETTER PHRASE

than jet lag. Jet lag sounded so harmless. "Oh, I'll be okay in a little while. I just have a touch of jet lag."

What Tom Moore felt wasn't jet lag. This was something more like jet flu, or jet attack, or maybe jet coma.

For almost twenty hours he had been on a series of planes.

A Little Piece of Paper

Moscow to St. Petersburg. From there to Munich. Munich to London. And finally on to New York. By the time the small government Starcraft jet taxied onto the tarmac at JFK, Tom had to look up at the sky to tell if it was day or night. He felt like someone had beaten him on the head with a rock or drugged his coffee. Or both.

As usual, there had been men in dark suits wait-ing as soon as he stepped from the plane. The de-briefing had gone smoothly. Tom's mission in Russia had gone reasonably well—despite a few setbacks and that botched rendezvous right before he'd left. And despite the fact that the whole trip had been overshadowed by memories of the time he had spent there in the company of his wife. The agency people weren't interested in Tom's memories. All they cared about were the dry facts. They wanted to know about the contacts he had seen and the timetable of the assignment.

Tom stayed awake long enough to accept dry con-gratulations on the completion of the latest mission, then fell into the backseat of a bland government-issue sedan and gave the driver directions to his latest apartment. Before the car even started to move, Tom fell into a gray haze.

Even in the backseat of the sedan, his mind was haunted by images of Katia. Moscow had been her home and the place where she and Tom first met. Going back there left Tom with a heavy weight of memories that clung to him like cobwebs. He wasn't even sure he wanted them to go away. Katia was gone. Memories were all Tom had.

At least he could still see his daughter, even if it did have to be at a distance. Meeting with Gaia wouldn't be safe for either of them, but Tom *had* to see her and make sure that she was all right. See Gaia. That thought cheered him as he climbed out of the car and walked the last couple of blocks to his apartment.

The apartment wasn't much, just a small one-bedroom place tucked above a corner fruit stand. It was far from fancy, but it provided an adequate base for Tom—especially since he was rarely in town. When he considered some of the other places he had called home over the last few years, it was practically paradise.

The fruit stand was doing slow but steady business. Tom waved at the owners as he walked around the building and made his way up the wooden stairs along the side. Even in December the air was scented by peaches and limes from the store.

Tom was nearly asleep on his feet, but he wasn't so tired that he didn't check the door before he went in. Before leaving, he had placed a small scrap of paper at the bottom of the door. Nothing special, just a little piece of newspaper that he had torn off and wedged against the door frame. If someone wasn't looking for it, they would never know it was there. Which was exactly what Tom was counting on. If someone had opened the door while he was away, the paper would have fallen out. He had fancier methods of detection available, but Tom was a great believer in simple methods.

He bent and inspected the door. The paper was still in its place.

Tom smiled in relief. The bed, and eight hours of solid sleep, were waiting inside.

Except.

Tom had his hand on the doorknob before something started to tickle at his brain. For a half a second his tired mind tried to sort out what was wrong. As he did, his fingers continued to turn the knob.

The paper was still there, so everything had to be okay. Only it wasn't because ... because ...

Because the paper was turned the wrong way.

Someone had been there. Someone had gone inside, done whatever they wanted, and come back out. They had been careful. They had seen the little scrap of paper and put it back. Only not perfectly.

The doorknob clicked under Tom's hand, and the door cracked open. For the space of a heartbeat he stood there, staring into the darkness on the other side of the door.

Instantly the sleepiness and exhaustion he had felt since leaving Moscow vanished. Before his heart could beat a second time, he had started to turn away. Before a half second had passed, the suit bag had slipped from his left hand and he was at the top of the stairs.

The explosion came before he could take another

step. There was no noise because the force of the blast instantly stunned his ears into silence. It lifted him, stole his breath in white-hot heat, then flung him downward like a singed rag doll.

He hit the bottom of the steps, bounced, and was instantly forced against the wall by an inferno wind.

When it was over, Tom fell. He fell down into darkness. And silence. And the smell of peaches.

Even Gaia had her limits. **about tonight**

SAM PUT HIS FINGER AGAINST THE
pawn and shoved it forward on its
rank. "It wasn't like I did anything."

"Yah." A black knight jumped
in from the side of the board to
trample the unprotected piece.

"I mean, sure, I thought about
someone else. I'll admit that."
Sam pushed his bishop toward the center of the
board.

The black queen slid up beside the bishop. "Der is
nothing wrong with thinking."

Sam reached for his one remaining
rook, hesitated, then drew back the bishop instead.
"Okay, maybe I even kissed someone else," he said.
"But that's not nearly as bad as what she did. Not even
close."

"Yah, of course." The knight jumped again, and the
rook left the field.

Sam scanned his diminished army and frowned.
He shoved another pawn toward the opposite ranks.
"And the first chance she gets, the very first chance—"

The black queen swept forward. "Dat is checkmate."

"It is?" Sam blinked and looked across the board.
Usually he had a good grasp of the board, but now the
chess game seemed as remote as another planet. He
had lost. Again. He unzipped his heavy coat, fumbled
in his pockets, and came out with a ten.

Zolov reached across the board and took the bill from his hand. "Thank you," said the old man. He stared down his long nose and studied the bill carefully, as if expecting to find a forgery. After the personal inspection Zolov held the ten up in front of two battered Power Rangers that sat beside the chessboard. "What you think?" he said.

Apparently the little plastic people gave their approval. After a few moments Zolov crumpled the bill and shoved it into the depths of his old tweed coat.

Sam shook his head and stared off across the frozen park. "I don't know. I thought maybe Heather really was the one. Now she's completely lied to me, and Gaia doesn't care if I live or not, so—"

"Be good to Ceendy, you," Zolov said suddenly. The old man's face reddened, and he waved an ancient, arthritic finger at Sam. "I like dat girl."

"Cindy?" Sam leaned back in surprise. "You mean Gaia?"

Zolov's bushy eyebrows drew together. "Dat girl, you should be lucky to have her." The old Russian glared at Sam for a few seconds longer, then picked up his chess pieces and began to put them back into position for a new game. "She is not like the others."

Sam tried to think of something to say. He couldn't be sure—maybe Zolov was thinking of Gaia, maybe he was thinking of someone else entirely. Maybe he was

81

thinking of someone who had been gone for half a century. Zolov was never very clear on much. Except for chess. When it came to chess, Zolov was still as sharp as ever.

The Russian finished arranging the pieces and looked over at Sam. If the old man had been angry before, there was no trace of it remaining on his face. "We play again, yah?"

Sam did a quick calculation. Considering the difficulty he was having concentrating on the game, he was sure to lose. Even on his best days he could rarely match Zolov. But he could afford to lose another ten, and he certainly had nowhere better to go. "Sure," he said.

Zolov held out his hands. Sam picked one at random. The Russian unfolded his fingers to reveal a white pawn. "So," he said. "You go first."

Sam started playing again, moving the pieces through a standard opening. He glanced across the board and decided to risk Zolov's anger. "What is it that makes Gaia different?" he asked.

Zolov snorted. "You not know that, you not know Ceendy, do you?" He jumped a knight over a rank of pawns.

Sam had to smile. He still couldn't tell if Zolov was talking about Gaia or just talking. But this was better than sitting around brooding about Heather. "I guess Gaia is special."

Zolov grunted and shoved a pawn forward.

Sam studied the board for a moment before moving in reply. Just because he knew he was going to lose didn't mean he wanted to make it easy. "It doesn't matter how special Gaia is. She isn't mine."

Zolov started to move, stopped, and looked across the board at Sam. "You don't know?"

"Know what?"

The Russian shook his head. "Think he is a smart boy, but he doesn't even know."

"Know what?" Sam repeated.

"Doesn't know Ceendy loves him." Zolov looked down, pushed up his queen, and smiled. "Dat is check!" he cried.

Music from Mars

AS EXPECTED, THE SNOW HAD WIMPED out again. No more than a dusting remained along the hedgerows that bordered the park. The parks department, which had absolutely no appreciation for snow, had already completely cleared the main paths. Still, Gaia couldn't find much to complain about. The clouds had broken, the day was bright, and she didn't have to spend it *(a)* going to school or *(b)* sitting around the brownstone with Ella.

Gaia was due to meet Mary by the central arch in half an hour, which gave her plenty of time to cross the park. Normally she walked fast no matter where she was going, but now she strolled along the path at a leisurely pace, watching the people as they passed and the kids slipping down the metal slides on the playground.

She was near the center of the park when she heard a scratchy, warbling music drifting along the path. It was a strange sound. Gaia could make out a man's voice, but the words and the tune were utterly alien. Like music from Mars. She picked up her pace and angled toward the source of the weird sound.

A few twists in the path brought Gaia to a small group of people and a contraption just as strange as the sounds it was making. Mounted on what looked like a large version of a kid's red wagon, the thing spouted odd, angled lengths of plumbing pipe and a cone that looked like it might have come from a large desk lamp. At the heart of the mess Gaia could just make out a large—and very old—phonograph.

The record playing on the device wasn't any easier to understand from close up than it had been from far away. The singer's voice rose and fell, and alien words poured out. Gaia couldn't tell what the man was talking about, but there was no mistaking the message. This song was sad. This song was lonely. The singer sounded like he had just discovered he was the only person left in the world.

Standing there in the park with her hands in her pockets and her face chilled by the cold breeze, Gaia knew how he must have felt. She'd felt that way for a long time. But instead of thinking of her mother, the image that appeared in Gaia's mind was Sam. What was he doing right now? Did *he* ever feel this lonely? Did *he* ever hear songs that made him think of *her*?

Gaia wondered if she should walk over to the chess tables. She hadn't played in a while, and she really should keep in practice. She might get a chance to talk to Zolov. She might even run into Sam.

That was ridiculous, of course. Sam was with Heather. He was not only with Heather, he was sleeping with her. And Gaia should know: unbelievably, she'd witnessed them having sex not once, but twice. Although she could be a glutton for punishment, even Gaia had her limits. It was time to accept that Sam was never going to be part of her life. It didn't matter how Gaia felt about him because Sam didn't share those feelings.

"Is this song really that sad?" asked a voice at her back.

85

Gaia spun to find Mary looking at her. "You're early."

"So are you," said Mary. She tilted her head a little to the side and looked at Gaia. "Is something wrong?"

"No, nothing." Gaia was embarrassed to find there were tears blurring her eyes. The combination of the music and her own thoughts of Sam really had been getting to her. Gaia blinked away the tears and smiled. "How did your shopping trip go?"

Mary's lips turned up in a wicked grin. "Great, of course. I found exactly what I need for tonight."

"About tonight," said Gaia. "I don't know—"

"Oh, no, Ms. Moore," said Mary. "You're not getting out of this." She took Gaia by the arm and drew her away from the phonograph cart. "Come on, let's get somewhere we can talk without yelling."

Gaia followed as Mary led the way toward the north end of the park, where a re-creation of the Arc de Triomphe loomed over the people strolling the paths. The music from the weird phonograph faded until it was only a melancholy hum in the winter air. "Where do you want to go?"

Mary waved a hand ahead. "Doesn't matter. Somewhere we can continue our conversation."

"Which conversation is that?"

"You know." Mary gave Gaia a sideways look. "The conversation we were having about your mother."

Gaia stopped dead in her tracks. Mary was the first

person she had ever told about her mother's death. Sharing had made Gaia feel better than she expected, but she was definitely not ready to say more. "That wasn't a conversation," she said. "That was a dare."

"I know," Mary said. "But I thought it might help you feel better to tell me more about it. I'm here for you, Gaia."

"There isn't any more to tell," said Gaia. Images of snow and violence danced on her brain for a painful moment. "I told you everything."

"Everything?" Mary paced back and forth on the sidewalk. "What about your dad? And how did you end up with the Nivens? And why was your mother killed?" She shook her head. "You've barely even started."

Gaia started to answer, stopped, opened her mouth to reply, then shut it again. The problem with most of Mary's questions was that Gaia didn't really know the answers. And even when she did know, there were still things she wasn't ready to tell. "The truth or dare game's over now," she said. "Let me catch my breath before we get into more."

Disappointment creased Mary's forehead, but she nodded. "All right," she replied. "It's just that it's all so . . . so . . . sad and . . . I wish I could help."

Sad wasn't the first word that came to Gaia's mind when she thought about her own life. *Try tragic. Heartbreaking.* "Let's try another subject. Tell me what you found to wear tonight."

Mary raised her chin and struck a pose. "Only something perfect."

"How nice for you," Gaia said with a laugh. "At least one of us will look decent."

"That's the really good news," said Mary. She held up her left hand and revealed a small plastic shopping bag. She let the bag dangle from the tip of her finger and swung it back and forth. "Now for the even better news. I found something for you, too."

"You bought something for me?" Gaia looked at the bag and got a tight feeling in her stomach. "Something to wear?"

Mary nodded. "Something perfect for tonight." She held the bag out where Gaia could take it. "Come on. Take a look."

Gaia squinted at the bag suspiciously. "I don't know about this. I don't think I should even go."

"You promised."

"That's what you say," Gaia replied. "I don't even remember you asking."

Mary shrugged. "So you were mostly asleep. A promise is still a promise." She held up the bag and gave it a little jiggle. "Just look."

Gaia took the bag and peeked inside. "What is it, a top?"

Mary sighed in exasperation. "It's a dress, of course." She grabbed the bag back from Gaia, reached inside, and pulled out the garment.

Gaia's eyes went wide. "You're sure that's a dress?"

"Absolutely," Mary said with a nod. She shook out the dress and held it up against herself. "It's a little black dress. A genuine LBD. A staple of any decent wardrobe."

"Your wardrobe, maybe." Gaia shook her head. "I don't think that's my size."

"It's exactly your size," said Mary. She held the dress toward Gaia. "It'll look great on you."

Gaia took the dress from Mary and stared at it. It made her feel a little queasy to think about wearing the thing. Not that she didn't want to. Gaia could imagine what Mary or another girl might look like wearing the dress. A normal girl.

"You wear that tonight," said Mary, "and every guy in the place will be looking at you."

Yeah, it'd be a regular freak show. "This thing doesn't even have any straps." Gaia turned the dress over in her hands. "What's supposed to hold it up?"

Mary laughed. "You are."

The thought of that was enough to make Gaia want to drop the dress. "Thanks, but no." She started to hand the dress back, but Mary pushed her hands away.

"You're not getting out of it that easy," Mary said. "You're going to wear that dress, and you're . . . you . . ." Mary's voice trailed off, and she stared off into the distance.

"Mary?" Gaia turned and tried to see what had upset Mary, but Gaia couldn't see anything but a handful of people walking along a path. "What's wrong?"

Mary continued to stare for a moment, then shook

her head. "Nothing. Nothing's wrong." She raised one hand and pushed her red hair back from her face. "I'm seeing ghosts. That's all."

Gaia frowned. "You're not still looking for Skizz, are you?"

"No, I—" Mary stopped and shrugged. "Maybe. I don't know."

Gaia wasn't sure what to say. She knew that Mary had been afraid of the drug dealer. And Mary had been right to be scared. Skizz really had tried to hurt her to get back the money Mary owed for drugs. But there was no reason to be scared of the dealer now. Gaia wasn't proud of the beating she had given him, but there was no way he would be a problem to anyone.

"Skizz is in the hospital," said Gaia. "You know that."

"Yeah, I guess so." Mary still looked doubtful. "It's just that this morning . . ."

"What?"

Mary shook her head. "Nothing." The grin returned to her face. "Let's get back to an important topic, like how you are so going to wear that dress tonight."

Gaia thought about it for a second. She could wear the dress. She would look about as attractive as a football player in a tutu, but she could wear it. "I think I'll find something else."

"You won't even try?" asked Mary.

"Not this time."

Mary's bright green eyes locked onto Gaia's. "Coward."

Gaia took a step back. "What?"

"You heard me," said Mary. She jerked the dress from Gaia's hands and shoved it back into the sack. "I buy you a great dress, and you don't even have the guts to wear it."

Anger started to tighten down on Gaia. "If it's so great, why don't you wear it?"

"Maybe I will." Mary narrowed her eyes. "At least I'm not too scared."

"I am not scared," Gaia said in a near shout. "Believe me, I'm not afraid."

"Yeah?" Mary held out the bag. "Then prove it."

ED WAS ON HIS WAY OUT THE DOOR

Checking with Undertakers

when the phone rang for the two hundred and thirty-seventh time that afternoon. He groaned. Every time his parents were gone, it seemed like he spent all his time answering junk phone calls.

He rolled across the kitchen, grabbed the phone, and started talking. "Look, this is an apartment. We don't need insulated windows. We don't need siding. I don't need insurance because I don't own a car, and I don't donate to anybody who calls me on the phone. Clear enough?"

"That's great, Ed," said the voice over the phone. "Now, are you ready to listen?"

Ed fumbled the phone, dropped it, caught it, and shoved it back against his ear. "Gaia?"

"I need a favor," said Gaia. There was a burst of music and background noise.

"What kind of favor?" asked Ed. "Where are you, anyway?"

"I'm at Eddie's."

"Who's Eddie?"

"Eddie's the restaurant," Gaia said. The music started up again, and Ed had to strain to hear her over the driving beat. "I'm here with Mary."

"Yeah?" In his mind's eye Ed had no trouble picturing Gaia and Mary. Gaia's hair was long and pale, buttery blond. Mary's was shorter, wavy, and copper red. Both of them were beautiful. Together the two girls were the hottest pair Ed had ever seen. Just a couple of days before, Gaia had kissed him. True, it had been an exceptional situation, but it had been a kiss. A real kiss. Right on the mouth. He wondered what Gaia was wearing. He wondered what Mary was wearing. Maybe Mary would—

"Ed? Ed, are you there?"

"Uh, yeah." Ed tried to shake off the daydreams and listen. "I'm here."

"There's something I want you to do for me."

"Sure. What is it?"

Gaia made a reply, but Ed couldn't hear her over a sudden increase in noise from the restaurant.

"What was that?"

"Skizz!" Gaia shouted into the phone.

"What?"

"Skizz. Mary's old dealer. I want you to find out where he is."

Ed stared at the receiver. "How am I supposed to do that?"

"Check the hospitals."

"Why would he be in a hospital?"

"Because," said Gaia, "I put him there."

"Oh," said Ed. Then, "Oh!" as he realized the meaning of what she had said. "You sure I shouldn't be checking with undertakers?"

"No. Or at least, I don't think so. If you can't find him, check and see what you can learn from the police."

Ed grabbed a pad from the kitchen counter and made a couple of quick notes. "Okay," he said. "I'll see what I can find. But remember what happened last time we tried to play detectives?"

"We're not talking about going up against a serial killer," said Gaia. "I just want to be sure this particular scuzzy drug dealer is still out of the picture."

"Gotcha. I'll see what I can find out." Ed cleared his throat. "So, Gaia. If I find some information, maybe we can get together and—"

"Thanks, Ed," said Gaia. "I'll check in soon." The phone clicked and went dead.

Ed hung the receiver back on the hook and scowled. "Great," he said to the empty kitchen. "One kiss and she thinks I'll do anything for her."

Then he pulled a phone book out of the cabinet and started to look up hospitals.

MARY HELD THE PHONE CLOSE TO

her mouth. "Aunt Jen? Can you hear me?"

She waited for the reply from the other end and frowned at the receiver. Clearly the tales of Mary's terrible drug addiction were still affecting the opinions of her favorite aunt. "Aunt Jen . . . Aunt Jen . . . Aunt Jen! Look, I'm okay. I'm not at a party. I'm at a restaurant."

Mary shifted around on one foot to see if Gaia was watching her. "Eddie's. *E-d-d-i-e-s*. It's near the campus. NYU, okay?"

She nodded as she listened to her aunt's reply. "No

With a K

party. No drugs. Just a greasy restaurant. I'm having a cheeseburger."

Even this information generated a lengthy response. Mary began to wonder how many people went back on drugs just because so many people pestered them about staying off. "Look, Aunt Jen, I only wanted to see if you found out anything about that stuff I brought you."

Mary listened for a moment, gritted her teeth, and squeezed her eyes shut. "Yes, I promise it has nothing to do with drugs. Can we please forget the drugs?"

Mary took another glance toward the table and saw that Gaia was looking at her. She cupped her hand over the mouthpiece and tried to speak as softly as she could in the noisy diner. "Yes, I know what the name Gaia means. Uh-huh."

Mary dragged a small pad of paper from her pocket. *Thomas Chaos,* she wrote on the pad.

The Moss Situation

LOKI DIRECTED THE LASER SENSOR at the window of Eddie's diner. In proper situations the device was a wonder. It could take the tiny vibrations that sound caused in the window and use those vibrations to re-create the original sounds. This was not a proper situation. The noise level inside the place made it nearly impossible to sort one sound from the sea of babble. With some difficulty Loki finally managed to locate the voice of the Moss girl.

". . . is Gaia . . . what that means . . . father . . ."

Loki lowered the device in frustration. It was clear that the girl was discussing Gaia, but he couldn't tell what she was saying. Not even Loki could bug every phone in the city.

The situation was becoming intolerable. The girl had information about Katia, and she had shared that information with others. Possibly several others.

Loki dropped the laser detector back into his pocket, took out his phone, and pressed a single button.

"Yes," said an emotionless voice from the other end.

"We'll have to move faster than expected on the Moss situation," said Loki. "She presents too much potential risk."

"I understand," replied the flat voice. "Measures will be prepared."

"You handle the aunt," said Loki. "I'll take care of the girl myself."

ELLA PICKED UP THE PHONE ON

Step Two

the first ring. "Yes?"

"Hi," said the voice from the other end. "This is Sam Moon. Is Gaia there?"

Ella smiled. Sam was a beautiful boy. Nearly perfect, in Ella's carefully considered opinion. He was far better than anything that Gaia deserved. "No, Sam," Ella said sweetly. "I'm afraid Gaia is out."

"Do you know when she'll be back?"

"Not until late. She's out on a date with her boyfriend."

"Oh."

Ella ran a lacquered nail down the side of the phone. This was working out so well. "Do you want me to take a message?"

"No. No, I guess not."

"Should I tell her you called?"

"No," said Sam. "Thanks."

The sadness in his voice was absolutely delicious. "You're welcome, dear."

Ella set the phone back on its hook and brushed her fingers through her scarlet hair. The call couldn't have gone better if she had planned it. Now it was time for step two.

His
fingertips
pressed into
her, pushing
her

her

own

heartbeat

against him.

"YOU LOOK GREAT."

Gaia squinted at the image in the mirror. "I look ridiculous."

Mary rolled her eyes. "Are you kidding?" She moved around Gaia, inspecting her dress from all angles. "I wish I looked half as good as you."

Gaia tugged at the top of the dress. "Half my size is more like it. This thing might fit you, but it's *way* too small for me."

"Are you nuts? It's a perfect fit."

Gaia turned away from the mirror in disgust. "Okay, you've seen me wear the dress. You have to know I can't go out in this thing."

"All I know is that it fits great, you look great, and you should wear it." Mary flipped back her red hair and studied Gaia for a moment. "But if you're too scared—"

"I'm not scared," Gaia said between gritted teeth. "Being scared has nothing to do with it."

Mary nodded. "You just don't want to be embarrassed."

"Exactly."

"You're afraid somebody will make fun of you."

"Right . . . I mean, no." Gaia drew in a deep breath and blew it out through her mouth. "I am not afraid."

"Good," Mary replied brightly. "Then you won't mind wearing the dress."

Gaia lowered her face into her hands and shook

her head. She wondered if being a sociopathic loner was really such a bad thing. On her own, she managed to get into fights only with armed criminals. Somehow that didn't seem nearly as disastrous as wearing this dress out in public. "Please tell me we're going somewhere that nobody knows me."

"Absolutely."

Gaia raised her head. "And we'll never go there again."

Mary shrugged. "If that's what you want. Wait till you get there before you decide something like that."

"Then all right, I may be crazy, but I'll wear the dress." Gaia went to the closet, pulled out her longest coat, and pulled it over the snug dress. "I'm not saying I'll stay long. Once everyone's had a good laugh, I'm leaving."

Mary shook her head. "You really don't see it, do you?"

"See what?" asked Gaia.

"Believe me. When the guys see you in that dress, there is not going to be any laughing." Mary pulled her coat on over the translucent top and short black skirt that made up her own outfit. "Let's get moving."

Gaia wasn't afraid. She *couldn't* be afraid, but she was definitely not looking forward to this evening. Her mood wasn't improved when she saw that Ella was waiting for them at the bottom of the stairs.

Ella folded her arms and leaned back against the stair rail as the girls approached. "Well," she said. "And where are you two going?"

"Dancing," Mary answered before Gaia could open her mouth. "Want to come along?"

Gaia winced. She could read the sarcasm in Mary's voice. She had no doubt that Ella heard it, too. But that didn't mean Ella wouldn't say yes just because she knew how much Gaia would hate it. Gaia looked back over her shoulder and glared at Mary, but Mary only smiled in reply.

Ella gave a short laugh. "I do love to dance," she said, "but no. I'm afraid I have my own duties to attend to tonight."

"That's too bad," Gaia said quickly. "Well, I'll see you later."

She started to step past, but to Gaia's surprise, Ella reached out and laid her hand on Gaia's arm. "Do be careful, dear," she said.

Concern wasn't usual for Ella. "Sure. All right." Gaia walked on, and Ella's fingers slipped away.

"Please tell me you weren't serious," Gaia whispered as she and Mary reached the door.

"What? About Ms. Niven coming with us?" Mary grinned. "It would be something, wouldn't it? I'd love to see if she even can dance on those heels she wears."

"It would be something, all right," said Gaia. She pushed open the door and stepped out into the cold night.

It wasn't until she was outside the brownstone that Gaia realized how happy she was that Ella couldn't see what she was wearing under the coat. For the first time since she had come to New York, Gaia was wearing a shorter dress than her foster mother.

Oh my God. I'm dressed in Ella wear.

"TWENTY-THREE?"

Vodka

Sam nodded.

The woman behind the bar was thin and thirty something, with pink hair piled on her head, a neat gold hoop through the side of her nose, and deep lines around her eyes. She looked skeptically at the ID card, then at Sam, then at the ID again. "You look younger."

"It's a curse," said Sam. He reached out for the card, but the bartender pulled it away.

"I wish I had a curse like that," she said. She gave the card another long look and held it up to the light. "This is a good fake."

Sam jerked the card away from her and put it back in his pocket. "It's not a fake!" he said.

The woman held up her hands. "Hey, don't get so worked up. I didn't say I wasn't going to serve you." A phone rang. The bartender turned and picked it up.

While she talked, Sam spun around on his stool. There was a dance floor in the club, but no one was dancing. Not yet, anyway. Up on the stage a band was just beginning to set up and a couple of men were arranging lights. Sam wasn't sure what kind of music the band played. He thought about asking, but after a moment he decided it didn't matter. He hadn't come into the club for the music.

He pulled out the ID card he had used to get in. These days, with color laser printers, there was almost nothing that couldn't be faked. Making the ID hadn't taken ten minutes.

The bartender finished with her phone call and strolled back over to stand in front of Sam. "You're getting an awfully early start, kiddo."

"Sam."

"Whatever." The woman leaned one elbow on the bar. "What's it going to be tonight, Sam?"

Sam stuffed the fake ID down in his pocket and studied the bottles behind the bar. The range of beverages was a little intimidating. He wasn't a regular drinker. In fact, he usually skipped both the beer and the shots available at campus parties. He just didn't enjoy it that much.

But this time Sam wasn't drinking for enjoyment. He was drinking to take the edge off of Heather's betrayal. He was drinking to wash Gaia out of his mind. He was drinking to smother the pain that cut through him anytime he thought of either girl.

He expected it would take a lot of drinking.

Sam stared at the multicolored bottles for a few

seconds, then shook his head. "Give me a recommendation," he said.

The bartender took a bottle of water-clear liquid down from the shelf. "If I was you, I would go home," she said. "But if you're going to stay here, then go for vodka."

"Why vodka?"

"Because," said the bartender as she pulled out a glass and set it down on the bar. "Vodka is good when you want to do some serious drinking. It doesn't leave you with such a bad hangover." The woman tipped the bottle and filled the glass nearly full of the clear fluid. "And kid, you look like you're here for serious drinking."

ED HELD HIS FINGERS AGAINST THE

One Thing He Knew

bridge of his nose and tried to get his temper under control. "I *understand* you still need insurance information. I don't *have* insurance information. No. No. No! I don't know his Social Security number!" He listened for a moment longer, then slammed the phone back into its cradle.

Four hours before, Ed had been on his way out of the house. Instead of leaving, he had been on the phone for hours. He never even got out of his kitchen.

Ed had been trying to get information from St. Vincent's, where Skizz was staying, by pretending to be everything from the police to Skizz's brother. The workers at the hospital weren't stupid, but they were overworked. If you kept at it long enough and pestered hard enough, you could get them to tell you what you wanted. But it sure took time.

Ed glanced toward the windows and saw it was already dark outside. He thought about going out. He could find something to eat. Wander down to see what was on at the movies.

But the sad truth was, despite all the time he had spent badgering people over the phone, Ed still didn't have all the information he needed. He had the first part. It wasn't much, really, just a sentence or two.

And Ed knew one thing for sure—what he had learned so far wasn't going to make Gaia happy.

Why People Dance

"COME ON!" MARY TOOK GAIA by the hand and started dragging her toward the dance floor.

Gaia put on the brakes. "Wait."

"Wait for what?" Mary let go of Gaia's hand and swayed from side to side in time to the music. "Come on. Let's get out there."

People pushed past them on both sides. The band had been playing for only a few minutes, but already the floor was getting crowded with couples, singles, and assorted groups. The close press of people made Gaia feel more than a little trapped. She was used to being alone, prowling around the park or hiking down the streets at night. Being in the crowded nightclub made her so squeezed, that Gaia almost forgot about the way she was dressed. A l m o s t .

"Gaia!" Mary called. Even from two feet away she had to shout to be heard over the driving music. She spun around on her high-heeled shoes and flashed a bright smile. "Aren't you going to dance?"

Gaia shook her head. "I don't think so. Dancing isn't on my resume."

Mary grabbed her hand again. "You know how. You just don't know that you know." She pulled Gaia toward the center of the floor.

Gaia let herself be pulled. First it was the skimpy dress. Now it was dancing. She wondered if a person could reach a complete overload of embarrassment. A pressure so strong that they collapsed inward, l i k e a star falling into a black hole.

Mary released Gaia's hand. She started to dance slowly, shifting her weight and letting her arms drift back and forth. "Here's the secret," she said. "Guys have to learn how to dance. Girls don't. I mean, sure you have to learn if you want to be really good, but if you just want to have fun and get the guys bothered, all any attractive girl has to do is move."

Gaia looked down at her own feet. "That's great for attractive girls. How does it help me?"

Mary stopped dancing and put her hands on her hips. "Gaia, give it up. You know you're gorgeous."

"I'm not—"

Mary waved at the dancing crowd. "There's not a woman in this place half as hot as you. Why don't you want to believe that?"

"Because it's not true," said Gaia.

Mary frowned. "Then pretend, okay? For tonight just pretend that you're as pretty as . . . as . . . oh, as pretty as you really are!"

The tempo of the music picked up. Mary smiled and started moving again, swinging her hips and moving her body with the beat. "Come on, dance."

Gaia watched Mary for a few seconds. The red-haired girl moved so well. Her pale face and arms seemed to float above her dark clothing. She wasn't doing anything fancy, but her movements were smooth, fluid. The easy way Mary moved her body made Gaia feel jealous. There was no way she could move like that—and no way she would look as good as Mary did.

108

For long seconds Gaia stood still in the middle of all the dancing. She thought about leaving the floor. She thought about leaving the whole club. Then she thought about what Mary had said.

Gaia knew that Mary was only trying to make her feel better. She knew she wasn't beautiful—her mother had been beautiful, but not Gaia. But what if she was to pretend? Could she think of herself as beautiful for just one night? Could she imagine what it would be like to be a normal girl? An attractive girl without monster legs? A girl like Mary who knew how to dance.

She closed her eyes. Slowly Gaia began to move. Her feet remained almost still, but her legs moved. Then her hips. Then her body and shoulders and arms.

At first she felt awkward, stiff. Gaia knew how to move smoothly—she had gone through a thousand karate training exercises that were more about moving well than hitting anything. But dancing was different. There was no plan, no path to follow. She had to make it up as she went along.

Gaia picked up speed, bringing herself in time with the music. She started to feel a little better. A little looser. She was sure that if she opened her eyes, half the people in the club would be laughing at her. So she kept her eyes shut.

The more she caught up to the music, the more

she could feel it inside her. The drums pounded in her stomach. The guitars sliced along her arms and legs, driving her to move faster, to dance wilder. With her eyes still closed, Gaia raised her hands over her head and spun around.

Maybe everyone was laughing, but it was starting to feel good. Really good. The movements of her body became more confident. There was a jazzy, electric feeling in her limbs. It was something like the buzz she sometimes got before a fight.

When Gaia dared to open her eyes, Mary was gone. Lost somewhere in a sea of dancing bodies. No one was laughing.

But there was someone looking at her.

A young Hispanic man with flashing black eyes and short-cropped hair was dancing right in front of Gaia. He was smiling at her. And he was dancing at her.

The man wasn't very tall, barely as tall as Gaia, but he was well built, with a narrow waist and broad, square shoulders. Gaia guessed he was somewhere in his early twenties. He wore a black jacket that was hanging open at the front and a snug white shirt that pulled in tight against the brown skin at his throat. He was muscular. Not overmuscled, but smooth, firm, fit.

The man didn't say a word, but his eyes never left Gaia. He looked into her face as he danced. Right into her eyes.

Gaia could barely feel herself moving. It was like she was riding the music. It seemed effortless now, like something she had done all her life.

The tune ended, and the music changed, but Gaia never missed a step. For the first time in a long time she felt like she was part of something bigger than herself.

She understood why people danced.

The man moved closer. He leaned toward Gaia, and she leaned away—but not far away. They moved together, so close that the man's jacket brushed against the cloth of Gaia's dress. As soft as a whisper. Gaia's long blond hair sprayed around her shoulders and spilled across the man's face.

Their bodies were inches apart. Less than an inch. Touching. Gaia could feel the heat coming from the man's skin as if there were a furnace in his chest. She couldn't tell if the beat she felt was the music. Or her own heartbeat. Or his.

The man's hand moved around Gaia and settled at the small of her back. His fingertips pressed into her, pushing her against him.

In that moment Gaia forgot that she was wearing a dress that exposed her bulky legs and arms. She forgot that she was supposed to be embarrassed. For that moment she even forgot about her father, and mother, and Sam.

And when the song ended and the man—the man

111

she had never seen before in her life—brought his face down to hers, Gaia kissed him. Hard.

HOT IN THE THROAT

VODKA DID PACK A PUNCH. Unfortunately, that punch didn't hit Sam where he wanted. Instead of thinking less about Heather and Gaia, every shot of vodka only seemed to make him think about them more. And it burned more, as if he were pouring the alcohol straight into a raw wound in his heart.

Still, Sam didn't stop. He was sure that if he only drank enough of the cold, clear liquid, he wouldn't be able to think at all.

Sam leaned over the bar and waved an unsteady hand toward the glass. " 'Nother one," he said.

The pink-haired bartender gave him a quick inspection. "You sure about that, Sam my man?"

"Sure," Sam repeated with a nod.

The woman frowned. "All right, but just one more." She refilled the glass and waited while Sam shakily counted out the cost of the drink. "Whoever she was, she must have hurt you bad."

A girl with short, honey blond hair, big silver earrings, and a very small red T-shirt dropped onto the stool next to Sam. She gave him a quick smile as she ordered a beer. "Great band, huh?"

Sam glanced over the sea of dancing people at the trio up on the band platform. He shrugged. The truth was, Sam had barely noticed the music. Ever since his second drink, all the noise in the place had merged into a kind of hum. Even though the music was loud enough to send ripples across his drink, the vodka kept Sam insulated from everything going on around him. The music seemed dull and distant, like something happening in another town.

"They're okay," he said. "I guess."

The blond girl's smile slipped a bit. "You here by yourself?"

Sam nodded. He picked up his glass and took a drink. The vodka was cold in his mouth but hot in his throat. "All alone."

"Aww, that's too bad." The girl looked him over for a moment, then held out a hand. "Why don't you come out and dance with me?"

Sam started to say no. After all, he was supposed to be with Heather, and that meant not being with anyone else. Then he realized how completely stupid that was. There was nothing wrong with a little dancing. Besides, dancing was nothing compared to what

Heather had done. He certainly wouldn't be cheating on anyone.

But when Sam started to get up, the room began to swirl around him and the floor swayed like the deck of a ship caught in a storm. He stumbled back against the bar, tried to take a step, and stumbled again.

The girl put a hand on his arm. "Man, you're crashed."

"Am not," Sam replied. He tried to stand up straighter, but that only made the room start to spin faster.

The girl laughed at him. "I don't think you're going to be doing any dancing tonight."

Sam frowned. "I can dance."

"Sure, you can," said the girl, "but not with me. Next time hit the dance floor before you hit the bottle." She drained her beer, gave Sam a quick wave, and charged back out onto the dance floor.

Sam watched her go and felt a fresh flood of despair. He carefully sat down on his swaying bar stool and picked up his drink. He was going to be alone forever. That was clear.

He was beginning to think about leaving when someone new settled in next to him. It was a girl—no, a woman, a definite woman—in a skintight emerald green dress. The dress was cut very high on her thighs to reveal long, shapely legs, and it scooped down low at the top to reveal even more pale skin.

Long seconds went by before Sam could manage to raise his eyes from what the dress revealed and look up at the woman's face.

She smiled at him. "Hello." Her lips were very full and very red.

"Hi," Sam managed. He ran a hand across his tangled hair and tried to return the woman's smile.

"So why is someone as cute as you sitting over here all alone?" she asked. Her voice was soft. Throaty. Sexy.

Sam had to swallow hard before he could reply. "It's, um, a long story."

The woman leaned toward him, revealing even more of the contents of her dress. "That's all right," she said. "I've got all night."

ED SCRIBBLED DOWN A NOTE.

The Good Detective

"Thanks, Detective Hautley. That story will be in the paper tomorrow. Oh, absolutely. Page two or better. Yes, I have the spelling. Thanks again."

The phone went back on the hook for the last time, and Ed leaned back in his chair. He had lied so often that night that he felt like he had taken a crash course in method acting. He could probably go to work on Broadway. Or head out to Hollywood.

Or make a real killing ripping people off with a phone scam.

It had taken more hours of pretending to be someone he wasn't, but finally all the lying had paid off. All it took was finding the right person.

The right person turned out to be Detective Charles Hautley. Hautley was a vice cop who wanted to be in homicide, and he was willing to share a few choice details with a reporter who might make the poor, hardworking, clean-living detective into a star. Once Ed got the good detective on the phone, it hadn't taken him ten minutes to find out what he wanted.

Hautley knew all about Skizz. He knew the man's record. He knew about the dealer's trip to jail. And most important, he knew where Skizz could be found.

And now that Ed knew the answer, he wished he had never asked.

I always knew that vacation was
the best idea in the history of
the world. Right up there with the
doughnut.

You have to wonder who came up
with something so brilliant. It's a
shame that this hero isn't in the
history book. There should be stat-
ues. There should be parades. They
ought to give a holiday in honor of
the guy who came up with vacations.

Maybe there was some caveman
out there who got tired of hunting woolly mammoths. Better yet,
maybe it was some cave woman
stuck back home, chewing on
mastodon blubber and sewing
bearskins. One day she wakes up,
looks around, and says, "Hell
with this—I'm going to Florida."
One smart cave woman.

Even little vacations are
good. Memorial Day. Columbus Day.
Dead Presidents' Day. But when it
comes to vacation, size definitely matters. Spring break,
good. Christmas break, also good.
Summer, very, very good.

That's all I knew about vacation until last night.

But I have made a discovery every bit as important as that sun-bathing cave woman's. Something right up there with fire, electric lights, and Krispy Kreme. I have found the New World of vacations.

Ever hear someone say, "Wherever you go, there you are"? Yeah, it's a stupid saying. Corny. Stupid and corny.

It's also wrong.

Here is my attempt at explanation.

Point 1. I was at the club last night.

Fact B. Gaia Moore got left behind.

I don't want to sound like one of those guys selling self-improvement books on 3 A.M. infomercials, but you really can take a vacation from being you. You can stop worrying about who's looking or who's talking about you or what they might say. Why should I care what anybody there thinks of me? I mean, I don't have to live with those people. I probably wouldn't like them if I did.

If you run hard enough, you can outrun yourself. And the only secret is: Stop running.

Doesn't make any sense, right? That's because you haven't been there.

Actually, I can't claim solo credit for this great, world-shaking discovery. It was Mary Moss who blazed the trail to this hidden continent of vacation. It's because of her that I learned how to stop being Gaia for a few hours and just have fun. She led me to the land of Moss. Mary Land. The place where you don't stress over what other people think.

All my life I've never been afraid, but I think this is what it really means to be fearless. It means doing the things you

want to do without worrying about
being rejected.

So I think it's time to do
something I've been wanting to do
for a while. I think it's time to
talk to Sam.

The real
difference
this morning
was that
Gaia sounded
happy.

gaia

moore

naked

GAIA CAME OUT OF THE SHOWER

The Girl in the Mirror

with one of the tunes from the night before running through her head. She walked across the bedroom wrapped only in a towel, but she had a hard time walking. Her feet still wanted to dance.

She had started to rummage through the clothes beside her bed when she noticed the black dress thrown across her chair.

I wore that. I went out in public in that.

No one had laughed. At least, if someone had laughed, Gaia didn't notice them. The guy she had danced with—Inego, his name was Inego—certainly hadn't been laughing.

Gaia paused, stood up, and walked across the room to the mirror. Carefully she studied her reflection in the mirror.

Gaia wasn't prepared to admit that Mary was right—no way was she beautiful. Not by a long shot. Still, maybe things weren't so bad as Gaia had always thought. Sure, her legs were packed with muscle. But were they so awful? Her shoulders and arms were bulked up, too, but this morning they didn't look so terribly hulkish.

Gaia tried to imagine what it would be like if she

didn't know that girl in the mirror. What if she were just to meet this girl on the street or maybe at school? What if she didn't know this was Gaia Moore, fearless expert in all things kung fu and girl freak? Would she really think this blond stranger looked that bad? Could she be normal? Could she even be . . .

The phone rang. Gaia was across the room in a flash, leaving her towel behind as she ran. She grabbed the receiver and, for once in her life, managed to answer before Ella could get to the phone downstairs. "Hello," she said.

"Gaia?"

"Ed!" Still naked and damp from the shower, Gaia threw herself back onto the unmade bed and lay facing the ceiling. "How are you? It's a beautiful morning, huh?"

There was a pause of at least five seconds before Ed spoke. "It's cloudy outside."

"Whatever," said Gaia. "How are you doing?"

"I'm not sure," Ed replied. "I was trying to reach a girl named Gaia."

"That's me."

"Gaia Moore?"

"Don't be an asshole, Ed."

"Hmmm," Ed replied. "That sounds more like it. Okay, maybe I did reach the right girl after all. But you sound different this morning."

Gaia sat up on the bed and ran her fingers through her damp hair. "Different how?"

"I don't know. You sound cheerful, and you're not, I don't know—"

"Not what?"

"Not whining, I guess."

Gaia scowled at the phone. "I do not whine."

"Oh, yeah? Whenever you talk about your foster parents, or Sam, or school, or—"

"Shut up, Ed." Gaia bounced up from the bed, jammed the phone between her shoulder and her ear, and started digging through the available clothes. "If you're so tired of me, you could always call someone else."

ED SHOOK HIS HEAD, THEN REALIZED

that shaking your head didn't work when the other person was on the phone. "No," he said. "The Gaia report is the high point of my day."

Dancing Gaia

"All right, then," Gaia replied. "Stop complaining. Or should I say, stop whining?"

Ed grinned. Gaia did sound different, but she was still Gaia. The real difference this morning was that Gaia sounded happy. That was a condition that didn't happen nearly as often as it should. In Ed's opinion, Gaia needed to be happy all the time. And of course, the way to see that Gaia was happy all the time was to see that she fell in love with Ed.

He started to say something else, but his voice caught, and his smile collapsed. Gaia was happy.

And he was about to ruin it.

"Ed? You still there?"

"Yes." Ed cleared his throat. "I'm still here."

"Hang on for a second. I need to get something on. I'm standing here naked."

Ladies and gentlemen, Ed's mental theater presents: Gaia Moore Naked. *Now held over for another extremely popular extended run.* Ed considered it an absolute tragedy that the picture phone had never caught on. He thought of telling Gaia that there was no reason for her to get dressed just to talk on the phone, but he didn't want to give her quite that clear a glimpse into the things that churned in his brain.

"Okay," she said after a few moments. "I'm back."

"So, uh, did you and Mary go to the club last night?"

"Absolutely."

"And what did you do while Mary danced?"

"What do you mean, what did I do?" Gaia shot back, doing a pretty decent imitation of Ed's tone. "I went dancing."

"You?"

125

"What? Is it so shocking that I can dance?"

Actually, it wasn't shocking at all. It was very easy for Ed to imagine Gaia dancing. She had those incredible long, strong legs. `Dancer's legs`. In his mind Ed could see Gaia spinning and swaying on those legs. Her blond hair flying. He knew without ever seeing it that Gaia would be an incredibly sexy dancer.

"So," she said. "Do want to hear about it?"

"Sure." *Hearing might not be enough,* Ed thought. *How about coming over and doing a demonstration for me?*

Ed listened as Gaia described going to the club, getting out on the floor, and starting to dance. Every word increased the heat that was growing inside him. He could picture it in his mind almost as if he were really there. A new feature debuted in his personal Gaia Moore multiplex. `Dancing Gaia`. Of course, in real life Gaia had probably worn clothes while dancing, but Ed thought he could allow a few special effects in his mental movie.

"And when I opened my eyes," Gaia continued, "this guy was there."

The film suddenly broke in Ed's internal cinema and went flipping around the reel. "Sam?"

"No, not Sam. Some guy I never seen before."

"How bad did you hurt him?"

Gaia made a disgusted sound. "I don't automatically hit every guy I meet. I didn't hurt him. We danced together."

"You danced with a strange guy?"

"Did I mention he was really good-looking?" said Gaia. "And he was a really good dancer. We danced together all night. It was great. Maybe better than great. Incredible. I never really . . . I mean, I never danced like that before."

Ed felt a stab of jealousy. He was immediately jealous of any guy who spent time with Gaia. Having Gaia say that the guy was good-looking only opened that wound a little wider. But what really hurt, what really poured the salt into the cut and rubbed it in good, was the fact that Gaia and this good-looking stranger had danced together.

Ed lusted after Gaia twenty-four hours a day. He was pretty sure that he even loved her. One of these days, if he could show her what a great guy he was and stay close, Gaia might even start to love Ed. After all, she had kissed him, even if it was only once. All he had to do was keep at it and wear down her resistance.

But one thing Ed would never be able to do was dance with Gaia. He would never get to be with her the way the guy from the club had been the night before.

There was a new threat here, a threat maybe even bigger than the hurdle of Sam Moon. It was clear that Gaia liked the dancing. And the guy. If she kept going to the clubs, it would mean she saw less of Ed. And more of the guys who were there—guys who could dance.

"Ed?" Gaia called from the other end. "Are you still there?"

"I'm here." The wheelchair suddenly felt very hard

against his back and arms. He adjusted his position, trying to get more comfortable. "So, are you going to see this dancing fool again?"

"No," said Gaia. "At least, I don't think so. I didn't even tell him anything but my first name."

Good. The situation wasn't completely out of control. "So you just left. You and Mary."

"Are you trying to ask if I had sex with this guy?"

"No." *Yes.*

"Well, I didn't. We talked a little bit. And kissed a couple of times. But mostly we danced."

Kissed.

Ed felt like someone had roped a brick to his heart and thrown it in a lake. Gaia had kissed this stranger. Kissing wasn't supposed to be a big deal. People kissed all the time. But Ed had thought Gaia was different. He'd thought that the kiss she had given him was special. Important.

"Ed? You keep going quiet on me. Are you doing something?"

"No." Ed was embarrassed to hear the catch in his voice. "No, just thinking."

"Don't hurt yourself. What's the news? Did you find out anything?"

Ed had almost forgotten the reason for his call. He held the phone away from his face for a second and cleared his throat before speaking. "Yeah," he said. "Yeah, I found out something."

"So, is Skizz still in the hospital?"

"No." Ed picked up a piece of paper and looked at the notes he had scribbled the night before. "According to the nurse I talked to, his injuries weren't as serious as first believed. Plus the guy had no insurance, so they kicked him out."

"I'm not sure whether I should be happy or upset that he's not that hurt," said Gaia. "If he's out of the hospital, I guess he's in jail."

"That's the really fun part," said Ed. He flipped over his page of notes. "It seems that the drugs found on your boy Skizz were judged to be the product of an illegal search. Inadmissible as evidence."

"So how are they going to keep him in jail?"

"They're not," Ed replied. "Skizz is loose."

The Father of Gaia

MARY BENT DOWN AND PICKED UP A broken piece of wood. It was no more than a few inches in length, splintered at both ends, and scorched black. It was all that remained of the door to the apartment leased in the name of Tom Chaos.

"So what did he look like?" she asked.

The fruit stand owner scratched at his thinning hair. "I'm not sure I ever met the man," he said.

"Didn't you rent the place to him?"

The man nodded. "I did, but that was over the phone. I never met this Chaos guy in person." The man's face pulled down in a heavy frown. "If I knew what he looked like, I'd be putting up posters. This bastard blew up my stand."

Mary looked across the pile of rubble. "I thought the paper said it was a gas explosion."

The fruit stand owner snorted. "Oh, yeah, some gas explosion." He waved a thick finger at Mary. "That damn apartment didn't even have gas."

"So what—"

"Who knows." The man kicked at a pile of shattered boards and rotting fruit. "You gonna hang around here, you be careful. I got enough troubles with the insurance guys already." He turned and stomped away.

Mary looked at the ruined fruit stand and the shattered remains of what had once been an apartment. There wasn't much left. The fruit stand had been split down the middle. No one had been killed, but the building was twisted in its frame like a broken toy. Bricks from the back wall had landed as far as two blocks away. Only some of the plumbing still remained where the apartment had been, sticking up into the sky like the picked-over skeleton of some dead beast.

130

No one had been killed here, and there had been few witnesses to the actual explosion. It was a small story, buried deep in the pages of the *Times*. Except for the search that Mary's aunt had made, it might have stayed buried.

Mary pulled out her notebook and looked at the few lines she had scribbled. Thomas Chaos had rented the broken apartment. Gaia's father's name was Thomas Moore. There was no real connection. Only two little facts had made Mary come to the site of the ruins.

First, Thomas Chaos didn't exist. All the information he had provided in renting the apartment had turned out to be fake.

Second, in some versions of Greek mythology, Chaos was the father of Gaia.

If those two bits of information fit together as Mary thought, it made for interesting results. Gaia Moore's father was somewhere in New York.

That was information Mary thought Gaia might find very interesting.

It's supposed to be a dream. In fact, it's supposed to be the classic dream, something every male in America fantasizes about.

You're sitting alone when this beautiful woman walks up and sits down beside you. You might be drunk enough to think any woman looks good, but you're not drunk enough that you don't recognize gorgeous when you see it. True, this woman might be a little older than you, and she might be a little more slutty than your usual taste, but isn't that part of the way the dream works? This is a woman with a lot of experience when it comes to sex.

This beautiful woman— beautiful, sexy woman—starts to talk to you. She tells you you're cute. She says she likes you. She tells you she's all alone. She puts her hand on your leg. She brings her face so close, you can smell the flavor of her lipstick. And eventually she asks you if you want to go home with her.

What are you going to say?

So, the two of you end up in a hotel room, and the dress comes off, and she's just as sexy as you thought she would be. Her body is incredible.

She's as experienced as you thought she was. She knows exactly what do with her hands. And her mouth. And her body. Even if you're half drunk—even if you're ninety-nine and nine-tenths percent drunk—you're not falling asleep on this performance. She moves like no one you've ever met. She bends in places you didn't even know human beings had joints. She keeps you going not just once or twice but until exhaustion catches up with drunk and the room spins. When you fall asleep, she's still pressed against you. Warm, and soft, and sexy.

When you wake up, the woman is gone. There's no note. The hotel room is taken care of. There are

no obligations or commitments.
You get one night of fantastic
sex with one unbelievable woman
and the price tag is zero. That's
the dream, right? The all-
American male sex fantasy.

So why does it feel so much
like a nightmare?

Mary had absolutely no doubt that someone had come to kill her.

The fear of dying

IT WAS AFTER NOON BEFORE SAM

The Real Dream

made it back to his dorm room. As soon as he was inside, he stumbled across the room and collapsed on his bed.

Either the bartender was wrong or Sam didn't have the typical reaction to vodka. If there were hangovers worse than the one he was feeling, Sam didn't want to know about it. Already he felt like someone had lifted the top of his skull, poured in a box of thumbtacks, and put the lid back on. Add in the family of gerbils that had taken up residence in his stomach, and Sam was ready to call the Mafia and see if he could hire a killer to come and shoot him.

Sam crawled up the bed until his face was smashed against the pillow and tried to keep his head from exploding. The drums down the hall were silent this time, but they weren't needed. Sam's heart was beating all on its own. On some scale, he knew that the hangover was getting better. The idea that he might actually live through it now seemed like a possibility—not that death wasn't still an attractive option.

The bone-crushing hangover might not have felt quite so bad if Sam hadn't also felt so guilty.

Heather cheated first.

That was true. In fact, once one partner had

cheated, could you even call what the other did cheating at all? Shouldn't it be like getting a free hit?

Of course, Sam had kissed Gaia when he was still supposed to be with Heather. And there was the little detail of his constant Gaia obsession.

Sam worked at trying to get the right feeling of justification, but he couldn't manage to find it. Even memories of the great sex he had experienced the night before didn't help. Sam couldn't get past the idea that the sex was wrong. Great, but wrong.

It didn't matter that Heather had cheated. Heather didn't know that Sam knew that she had cheated. And Sam hadn't said anything to Heather about breaking up. So no matter what Heather had done, they were still an official couple. Which made sleeping with the woman from the bar absolutely wrong. And all of that was way too much thinking to do with a hangover.

The whole thing didn't make a lot of sense. Sam knew that. He was acting like some character from a book. Real people weren't supposed to think like this. Real people slept around. Everybody said so.

But it didn't feel right. Maybe no one in the world would blame Sam for sleeping with this woman after Heather had cheated on him. Hell, every guy in the dorm would probably congratulate him for scoring

137

with this babe even if Heather hadn't cheated on him. It didn't matter. The only thing that mattered was that Sam felt guilty. What he had done was wrong, no matter how many talk show guests and frat dudes might disagree.

He was going to have to talk to Heather. He was going to have to tell her it was over.

There was a knock at the door.

Every rap of the mystery guest's knuckles went through Sam's skull like a chain saw. He winced and pulled the pillow tighter around his exploding head. "Go away!" he shouted as loudly as he dared.

"Sam?" said a faint voice. "Is that you?"

Sam groaned and rolled to the edge of the bed. The world did a little jumping, twisting lurch. "Who's there?"

"Gaia."

"Gaia?" Sam sat up quickly, bringing a railroad spike of fresh pain to his head. He couldn't imagine why Gaia Moore would be at his door. Especially not when she had been out with her boyfriend only the night before. He got up and stumbled across the room over a floor that pitched and heaved like a ship on the high seas. He fumbled open the door and saw that the impossible was true. Gaia Moore had come to call.

"Why are you . . . ," he started, then he swallowed and tried again. "Uh. Hi, Gaia."

"Hi, Sam." Gaia was dressed in usual Gaia gear, cargo pants and a gray sweatshirt, but there was something different about her hair. It almost looked like it had been combed. If Sam weren't drunk, he would have sworn she was blushing.

"I wanted to ask you something," she said.

"What's that?"

Gaia pushed her hair back from her face, glanced at Sam for a moment, then looked away. "I was wondering if you had anything planned for tonight."

"Tonight?" Sam wondered if this was just part of the hangover. Was it possible to have hallucinations from one night of drinking? If he didn't know better, he would have sworn Gaia Moore was asking him out on a date.

"It's New Year's Eve," said Gaia. "So I thought you'd probably be doing something with Heather."

"No," said Sam. "I'm not doing anything with Heather." In his own ears he could hear both anger and guilt in that statement.

"That's great!" said Gaia. "I mean, it's not great that you don't . . . I mean . . . I thought maybe you would want to get together tonight."

Sam felt a moment of dizziness that had nothing to do with his hangover. Gaia Moore *was* asking him out on a date. The last few days had been an incredible roller coaster. First there was the woman at a bar, now

139

this. His life was getting so strange in all directions. "Sure," he said. "Sure, I could do something tonight." Surely by then the hangover would have faded.

"Cool." For a moment Sam caught a glance of that endangered species, a Gaia Moore smile. "I'm meeting Ed and Mary around eight. If you came over around seven, we could walk over together."

"Ed Fargo and Mary Moss?"

"Uh-huh. We're talking about checking out the fireworks in the park. If the weather's not too crappy, we thought we might even do the whole tourist Times Square thing. After all, this is my first New Year's in New York."

Ed and Mary. Sam knew Ed Fargo well enough and had meet Mary Moss a few times. If Ed and Mary were coming along, then this wasn't so much a date as a kind of group activity. Nothing serious. Gaia might even be asking Sam more as a let's-be-friends kind of thing, not an I-love-you kind of thing. In fact, that seemed like what had to be going on. Ed and Mary were Gaia's friends. Gaia was just inviting Sam to be part of the gang, not to be her boyfriend.

"Sure," said Sam. "Sure. I'll be there." Being friends with Gaia was better than getting no dose of Gaia at all.

"All right," said Gaia. She bounced on the balls of her feet for a moment. "Okay. I guess I'll see you then."

"Right," said Sam. He managed to make what he hoped was a decent smile in reply.

Gaia hesitated for a moment. Then she spun on the soles of her worn sneakers and padded off down the hall.

Sam watched until the top of her blond head had disappeared down the staircase. Maybe for some guys, meeting a beautiful woman in a bar and having a night of sex was their fantasy. But for Sam Moon, Gaia was the real dream.

MAYBE I SHOULD LIE.

Ed stared at the phone and tried to rub away the headache that was building behind his eyes. He had spent so much time on the phone the last couple of days, his right ear felt hot and swollen. If the phone company charged for local calls by the minute, Ed would have been way deep into his college fund.

There was only one more phone call to make now, but Ed wasn't sure he should do it. If he dialed the phone, it would mean putting Gaia at risk. If he didn't dial, it could mean risking Mary.

I could check it out myself, he thought. *I could tell Gaia that I couldn't get the information. Then I could go up there myself and . . . and . . .*

And what? Ed might hate it when people thought he couldn't do something because he was in a wheelchair. But there were a few things that he really couldn't do. This might be one of them.

One dark, deep little part of Ed's brain definitely did not want to make this call. Sure, Mary was pretty. A little wild sometimes, but Ed liked her. And she was a friend. Still, Mary wasn't Gaia. Gaia was beautiful. Gaia had kissed him. He didn't just like Gaia—he was pretty sure he loved her.

The little reptile part of his brain was talking loud and clear. *Forget Mary. Don't do anything that would get Gaia in trouble.*

That reptile brain was hard to resist. The only thing fighting against it was the idea that if he didn't call, he would be breaking Gaia's trust. If he didn't call and Mary got hurt, Ed would have to live with that forever.

Still, it took a good ten minutes before he lifted the phone and reluctantly dialed Gaia's number.

"Hi. This is Ed. I need to speak to Gaia."

A few seconds later her voice came over the phone. "Hey. You going to be there tonight?"

"I'll be there," said Ed. He took a deep breath and continued. "But I found out something that I thought you should know."

"What's that?"

"I found Skizz."

142

A Great Agent Once

"ARE YOU SURE YOU DON'T FEEL up to it?" asked George.

Ella summoned up her best suffering-but-devoted-young-wife smile. "I'm sorry, dear. It really does feel like I have a cold coming on." She laid her fingers lightly against her chest. "I shouldn't make a trip right now."

George frowned. "If you're certain."

"I am." Ella nodded sadly, the brave smile still on her brightly painted lips. "You go on. I'll stay here, nurse my cold, and watch the celebrations on television."

George thought for a moment, then shook his head. "Nope. If you're staying here, I'll just stay with you."

Ella sat up quickly. "Now, George, you can't do that. You know you have commitments down in Washington."

"Those commitments can wait." George knelt down beside the couch, and took Ella's hand. "I'm more worried about us."

"Us? What could be wrong with us?" Ella looked at him with mock concern. "Is there something bothering you, dear?"

"What's bothering me is how little time we spend together," said George. Worry creased his forehead. "Half the time my job takes me out of town. And even when I am home, it seems like you have a photography assignment almost every night."

"I'm trying to get established," replied Ella. "It's important that I take any assignment I can get."

George squeezed her hand. "I understand that, but I miss you, Ella. I want to be with you."

Ella reached across with her free hand and patted George softly on the cheek. "Don't worry. We have all our lives to be together." She nodded toward the door. "Now, go on to your party. The last thing I want you to do is to stay here and catch my cold."

George nodded. "All right," he said. "I'll go. But when I get back, we're going to have some reserved time together."

"Wonderful," said Ella. "I can't think of anything better."

With one last look, George turned for the door. "Take care of yourself while I'm gone."

"Don't worry. I'll be waiting right here." Ella waved at him as he went out the front door of the brownstone.

As soon as the door closed, Ella's expression turned into a scowl. She climbed up off the couch and went into the kitchen to wash her hands. It was getting to the point where just the touch of George's hands was enough to make her want to scream. Just the sight of him made her stomach churn.

George Niven was a great agent once. Even Loki said

so. But he wasn't anymore. Now he was just weak and stupid. Ella wasn't sure how much longer she could keep up this charade. She had never expected to be with George this long. Loki had promised her that one day this long project would move into the next phase. When that happened, Ella wouldn't have to pretend anymore. Wouldn't have to be with a man she despised more every day.

At least she would get a chance to see Loki tonight. If she was lucky, she would even spend the night in his bed. Now that George was out of town, everything would be fine.

To: outsider@div13.gov
From: insider@div13.gov

ENCODED TRANSMISSION—256-BIT KEY TO FOLLOW

Request immediate meeting. Location delta. 1900 hours.

Situation degrading.

MARY LOOKED AT HERSELF IN THE

mirror and grinned. She didn't think she was the most beautiful girl in the world. Usually she didn't think much of her looks at all. But she had to admit that the camisole looked very fine.

Everyday Events

The flimsy top would definitely not meet with her mother's approval, but then, Mary's mother had already gone off to her own New Year's event. There was no one left in the house to pass judgment on what she was wearing.

Mary thought for a moment about changing into something else. After all, if they really did end up down at Times Square, this outfit was going to be beyond chilly. But she was also going to be standing next to Gaia Moore all night. Gaia might not realize she was beautiful, but to most guys, that only made Gaia more attractive. Unless she looked her very best, Mary could get overlooked.

She was still debating whether or not to change when the phone rang. Mary picked it up, expecting it to be Gaia or Ed. Instead there was only a crackling, humming sound on the line. The phone had sounded funny for the last couple of days. There was always this strange little hollow tone to everything. But this went way beyond the previous problems.

"Hello?"

"Mary . . . you . . . me." The voice was faint and filled with static.

"Aunt Jen?" Mary spoke into the phone. "Is that you?"

". . . trouble . . . Katia Moore . . ."

A chill ran down Mary's back. "Aunt Jen, there's something wrong with your phone. I can't hear you."

". . . government . . . secret . . ." Then the phone gave one last squawk and went dead in Mary's hand.

"Aunt Jen?" Mary called hopelessly into the silence. "Are you there?" She waited a few seconds, then set the phone down.

Her aunt must have been calling from a car phone. That was the only explanation. She must have gone into a tunnel and lost the connection.

It was clear that her aunt was trying to tell her something about the death of Gaia's mother. Mary was surprised that her aunt would be working on the problem so late on New Year's Eve. The information on Katia Moore must have turned out to be particularly interesting.

Mary stood by the phone for a moment, hoping her aunt might call back, but the phone stayed quiet.

Mary went back to getting ready, but the chill of fear that had arrived with the phone call wouldn't go away. It had to be more than an interesting story to keep her aunt working so late. If she was calling from a car phone, maybe she was on her way somewhere. Maybe she was even coming to talk to Mary in person.

Then Mary remembered a flaw in that theory. Aunt Jen didn't even *own* a car. She might have a portable phone, it sometimes seemed like everyone in Manhattan carried one, but there was no way the reception should have been so bad. Not from anywhere in the city.

Mary ran back across the room and picked up the phone. This time there was no strange hollow sound. This time there was no sound at all. The phone line was dead.

Mary's heartbeat was suddenly racing. She was paralyzed for a moment, the dead phone in her hand. One part of her brain was still trying desperately to fit this into the world of everyday events. Phone lines go out. It's New Year's Eve. A million people probably called each other at the same time and blew the circuits. But the rest of her mind didn't buy it.

She put the phone back on the hook and grabbed her coat from the closet. Gaia was expecting to meet Mary in the park. That was still an hour away, but Mary decided she would rather freeze out in the cold or walk over to Gaia's brownstone. Anything but stay here. She slipped into her coat, picked up her purse, and headed out.

Mary had gotten as far as the kitchen when she

noticed something strange. There was a little case lying on the kitchen table. A small, leather case that looked something like the case for the flute Mary had once played in junior high band. Curious, she walked over to the case and looked inside.

The case was packed with some kind of dense gray foam. There were cutouts in the foam just large enough to hold an assortment of objects. Only a few of the slots were full. Two held small objects the size of a fingernail. They looked something like miniature lollipops, slightly squashed lollipops, only inside the translucent balls Mary could see an array of tiny electrical parts, and where the stick should have been on a piece of candy, there was a bundle of wires.

Mary had never seen anything quite like this, but she immediately had an idea of what it was for. There had been a funny sound on the phone all week. Someone had been bugging her phone, listening in on every conversation.

There was an empty opening at the center of the case that was shaped something like a large cigar. Next to it was a shape that was considerably more frightening. There was no doubt about what it was meant to hold. Mary could make out every detail of the outline—the grip, the trigger guard, the long, slender barrel. The third opening was fitted to hold a gun, and that gun was missing.

But even that wasn't the worst thing in the case.

The worst thing was two small glass vials. One vial was still in its slot. The other of the tiny bottles was sitting out on the counter. Inside it was a thimble full of snow-white powder.

Cocaine.

The sight of it brought an unexpected wave of desire boiling up from somewhere deep in Mary's guts. It had been *so* long.

One quick sniff. One quick sniff and I'll be able to think this through so much better.

Mary took a slow step back. If there was any time in the world when it was a seriously bad idea to get cranked out of her head, this was the time. She shifted her eyes as far to the right and left as she could without turning her head.

Someone was in the house. That someone was carrying a gun. Mary had absolutely no doubt that someone had come to kill her.

THE CROWD ON THE F TRAIN WASN'T

the most upscale Gaia had ever seen. There was a high concentration of black dusters and guys with

Some Dogs

stubbly little beards. Even on New Year's

Eve, she suspected more of them were interested in getting drunk or getting high than in celebrating.

Perfect customers for Skizz.

Gaia rode in the front of the front car. If she could have, she would have ridden on the outside. She would have pulled or pushed or done anything to make the cars go faster. There was a tension in her legs. An ache in all her muscles. It wasn't fear, but it wasn't quite the same cold energy she felt right before a fight. By the time the train reached the station, the tension was so great that she squeezed out the door and flew up the stairs before anyone else on the train had taken two steps across the platform.

Skizz was loose. Gaia had expected the scumbag to spend a week or more in the hospital. After that, he should have gone to jail for pushing drugs. Mary should have been safe for years.

Now Gaia would have to take care of him. Again.

Gaia knew she could handle Skizz. She had already kicked his flabby ass twice. Three times would be no problem. That didn't mean there wouldn't be complications. There was no telling what kind of mood Skizz was in. Beating up a guy like Skizz was kind of like kicking a feral dog. He might get scared and run away. He might turn around and bite.

Gaia had one mission, one goal. She had to make sure that a simple message got through the dealer's lice-ridden head: Get near Mary Moss and die.

151

Gaia reached the street and cut across an intersection toward St. Mark's Place. It was nearly dark, and fat snowflakes were drifting down from a deep gray sky. The sun was still shining on the taller buildings, but already the air felt ten degrees colder.

There weren't as many people on the street here as there were back in the Village. The stores and restaurants along the sidewalks were at least a grade below those near Washington Square. Not the swankiest neighborhood in the city.

St. Mark's Place was a park, but it turned out to be considerably smaller than Gaia had expected, little more than a block of green space and a few knots of trees. Gaia stood in one corner of the cold space for a few minutes and watched as two men passed a bottle back and forth. Two girls with spiked hair walked past, and a cloud of pungent pot smoke momentarily swamped Gaia.

She didn't see Skizz.

According to Ed's source in the police department, Skizz had been spotted at this location twice in the last two days. Both times he had avoided arrest, but the park was a known site for drug traffickers. None of which guaranteed that Skizz would show up tonight.

Gaia bit her lip and did a slow scan of the people in the park. It was getting close to seven. Unless she wanted to miss her meeting with Sam, Gaia needed to get back on the train. It looked like lowlife hunting was going to have to wait for another night.

She was halfway back to the station when she saw a familiar shape on the street corner ahead. A big guy with a round gut and a big, jutting beard. Gaia smiled a hard smile. *Thar she blows.* There was no mistaking Skizz's bulky silhouette.

Gaia thought about her approach. She could go in cool and casual. She could come in screaming and kicking. She could be sneaky. Sneaky won.

She came up behind Skizz, grabbed him by the back of the coat, and pulled.

The man flew back a step, stumbled, and fell onto the dirty snow. Gaia quickly stepped around in front of him and put a foot on his chest. "Hi, there," she said. "Funny mee . . ." She stopped in midword.

She had the wrong guy. This wasn't Skizz. This couldn't be Skizz.

Only it was.

The drug dealer was a wreck. His face was lopsided and swollen. His lips were split, and inside his open mouth Gaia could see several broken or missing teeth. There was a cast on one of his legs and a sling around his left arm. A bandage wrapped his dirty hair. His left eye was covered by gauze and tape. His right eye looked up at Gaia with complete and utter terror.

"You," he croaked. "It's you." His voice shook.

Gaia couldn't feel fear, but she could feel shock. *I did this.* She didn't exactly feel sorry for Skizz. He had only gotten what he deserved. But it was a little stomach

153

twisting to see what she had done to a man using nothing but her hands and feet.

Gaia took a deep breath and tried to get the proper tone of mean back in her voice. "I came to make sure you stayed away from my friend."

Even as she said it, the statement sounded ridiculous. Skizz couldn't be the one who was after Mary. Skizz couldn't be after anyone.

The dealer pushed his hands against the ground and scooted himself back through the snow. "Don't," he blubbered through his torn lips. "Don't hurt me." Tears streamed from his one good eye and rolled into his matted beard.

Gaia stared down at him for a few seconds longer. Then she put her hands in her pockets and started walking for the subway station.

Some dogs ran. Some dogs bit. Some dogs got broken.

At least Gaia could be sure of one thing. Mary was safe.

MARY MOVED SLOWLY ACROSS THE

carpeted floor. At every step she paused and looked left and right. She could barely get herself to move. Her knees trembled, and

My Hero

her legs were unsteady. At any moment she expected a bullet to come out of some corner of the apartment. The fear was so bad, she wanted to lie down and just wait until whoever had left the case on the table came to kill her.

She froze at the door to her room and stood trembling there for several seconds, unable to move.

A noise down the hall broke her free from her paralysis. It was a faint sound, but it was enough to propel Mary through the door and into her room. She closed the door behind her and carefully turned the lock.

She didn't have any illusion that the door would actually keep the intruder out. Her parents had managed to open it with nothing more sophisticated than the bent end of a clothes hanger. And the door was thin enough that even Mary could have probably knocked it down with a kick. She only hoped it would buy her time.

Still trying to move as silently as possible, Mary crept across the room and gave the phone another try. No dial tone. Nothing.

That meant there were two choices. Mary could try to go out the front door. She had already passed on that option once. She figured that it was what the intruder expected, and now he would be even more prepared. Hopefully, whoever was in the apartment wouldn't be prepared for option two.

Before she made her escape, Mary had one more

little task. She went to the dresser and grabbed the handles for the lowest drawer. Mary pulled the drawer open slowly, an inch at a time. She held her breath. Any noise. Any noise at all might draw the stranger with the gun.

It took only a few seconds to open the drawer and grab the bottle of pepper spray she had hidden inside, but they were long seconds. The fear of dying seemed to stretch out time, making every moment into an hour.

Mary stuffed the pepper spray into her pocket and hurried across the room to the bed. Under the foot of the bed was a small case made of bright orange plastic. It was one of those stupid things that her parents had bought from some salesman. Some stupid thing that Mary had always thought was a waste of money. She had certainly never expected to use it. But she was glad she had it now.

Mary slipped the case from under the bed and popped open the latches on the sides. She shivered as the case opened with a loud click.

Inside, there was only a bundle of wire and thin metal rods. It looked like a mess, but Mary dragged it free from the case and carried it over to the window. Then, with her heart beating high in her throat, she put her thumbs against the window locks and pressed. There was a terrible moment when she thought the old locks wouldn't open, but a second later the locks popped, the glass shivered, and the window swung slowly inward.

A blizzard of cold air swirled into Mary's bedroom. Snow settled on her head. Wind made the clothes in her closet into dancing ghosts.

Carefully Mary leaned over the edge and looked down. Five floors below, cars hummed past on the street.

She looked at the bundle of wire and located the top. With hands that shook from both fear and cold, Mary hooked the top over the windowsill and hurled the rest out the window. The emergency escape ladder uncoiled with a whine. Far below, she heard the bottom of the ladder clank against the side of the building.

Mary put her head through the window again and looked down. The ladder didn't reach all the way to the sidewalk, but it was close. If she climbed down and hung from the bottom, her feet would be no more than a dozen feet from the ground.

But that climb didn't look too easy. In fact, it looked insane. The narrow ladder seemed as `fragile as a bit of spiderweb`, and the bitter wind made the whole thing bob and dance. If Mary climbed down the ladder to the bottom and dropped from there, she would probably be okay. But if she fell from the top, or from thirty or fifty feet up, the sidewalk would do the intruder's job as well as any bullet.

Mary stepped back from the window and looked at

the bedroom door. Maybe going out the front wasn't such a bad idea after all. Slipping past the gunman suddenly seemed like a much better idea than trying to climb that toy ladder down five floors.

The bedroom door rattled. The knob turned, stopped, then turned the other way. A moment later there was a clicking metal-on-metal sound.

Picking the lock. *They're picking the lock just like my parents used to do when I was sulking in my room,* she realized.

Without another moment's thought Mary was standing in the window. She grabbed the ladder, gave it a tug to see if it would hold, then started down.

The ladder was even more treacherous than it looked. The rungs were so narrow that they bit into Mary's fingers like knife blades. The way the ladder lay up against the side of the building made it nearly impossible to keep her feet in place. Again and again her toes slid from a rung, sending her on a dozen terrifying minifalls. But she was doing it. She was making it down.

The end of the ladder was twenty feet below. Then ten.

There was a sudden jerk from above. Mary looked up to see the silhouette of a figure leaning from her bedroom window. With impossible strength, that person was pulling up the ladder. Instead of going down, Mary was heading back up.

She scrambled for the bottom of the ladder, moving

as fast as she could, but by the time she reached the last rung, the end of the ladder was nearly twenty feet above the sidewalk. And it was getting farther away with every passing moment.

Mary let herself dangle from the very bottom of the ladder, closed her eyes, and dropped.

It seemed to take a long time to reach the ground. Too long.

The ground hit her like a subway train. A white-hot lightning bolt ran up Mary's right leg. She was on her side, then her face, then her back, then her side again. A sparkle of lights swam across her vision, and everything in the world shrank to a gray point far down a deep well.

When the world came back, Mary was looking at red taillights streaming past in the slushy street. Her face was lying in cold snow. The rest of her felt kind of numb, like that pins-and-needles feeling you get when your arms or legs fall asleep.

She tried to sit up, but that only brought a new explosion of pain from her leg. Mary bit back a scream and slowly turned herself over.

She was still alive. For the moment that seemed like a miracle.

"Miss?" A man came up at a run. "Miss, are you all right?"

Mary started to nod, then changed her mind. "No. I think my leg is hurt."

The man looked at her for a moment, then looked up at the building. "I saw you come down. That was quite a fall."

"Yeah, tell me about it." Mary squinted up at the window, but she could see no one looking down. The ladder was also missing in action.

"Is there a fire?"

Mary shook her head. "A guy broke into our apartment. I think he's trying to kill me."

The man stood and looked in both directions along the sidewalk. "I think you had better come with me," he said. "We should get you to the police."

Mary's long involvement with drugs hadn't exactly made the police her favorite people, but this seemed like an excellent time to make new friends. "Sure," she said. She tried again to get to her feet. Her right leg didn't cooperate. "I think I'm going to need some help."

The man reached down and helped her to her feet. "I have a car parked on the next block. You think you can make it?"

Mary nodded. "Let's go."

She hopped along at the man's side, leaning against him and keeping almost all of her weight on her left foot. As they passed under a streetlight, she saw that the man was older than she thought. Probably somewhere in his forties. He seemed strong, though, and he had a handsome, chiseled face.

160

"Why would someone be trying to kill you?" the man asked.

"I don't know," said Mary. She stopped for a second to catch her breath, then limped on. "There was this guy who tried to kill me a couple of days ago, but I don't think he has anything to do with this."

"Two different guys tried to kill you in the last few days?" The man gave a surprised laugh. "You're a popular girl."

"Mary," she said between breaths. "My name is Mary."

The man paused. He supported her weight on one arm and reached across with the other to shake her hand. "My name is Loki."

"Loki? Is that from mythology or something?"

"Exactly."

Mary shook his hand and smiled. "It's a weird name, but you're certainly my hero tonight, Loki."

He took the
dark, heavy
bulk of the
Glock pistol
and pressed
the blunt
barrel
against
Mary's back.

SAM RANG THE BELL ON THE FRONT

of the brownstone and waited. He was more nervous than he wanted to admit. *This isn't a date,* he told himself. *Gaia*
probably doesn't even think about me like that. She only invited me over as a friend.

That didn't do much to help. But at least he was going to get to see Gaia. Since Thanksgiving they had barely spoken. Her visit was the last thing he had expected.

He heard feet coming toward the door at a near run. There was a fumble of latches, and the heavy wooden door swung open. "Sam!" said Gaia. "You came."

"I said I would come," he replied.

"Yeah, but I figured Heather would call, and you would . . ." Gaia stopped and shook her head. "Never mind. Come on in while I grab my stuff. I just got back myself."

Sam followed her inside the brownstone. "Where have you been?"

"I had an errand to take care of," said Gaia. "But it's all worked out now."

Sam nodded and looked around the room. "This is a great place," he said. He looked up at the high ceilings and the heavy molding. The brownstone was authentic and well maintained. Except for some tacky ceramic figures and some modern art pieces that didn't fit the style of the house, it was the kind of a place that made it into the Sunday magazine section on homes.

"Thanks. It's okay," said Gaia.

Sam stopped looking at the room and looked at Gaia. "You look . . . different."

Gaia tilted her head. "If that was a compliment, you need more practice."

"It was," said Sam. "So I guess I do." Gaia did look different. Her hair, which often looked like it had never been introduced to a comb, was glossy and smooth. Her jeans and sweater were nothing fancy, but they were a lot nicer than the baggy cargo pants and sweatshirts that Sam had always seen her wear before. "So, where's the rest of the gang?"

Gaia opened a closet and pulled out a coat. "I told Ed and Mary we'd meet them in the park. We probably should get going."

"Okay," said Sam. He was relieved to hear that the list hadn't been expanded. If Gaia was worried that he might be doing something with Heather, Sam had been equally worried that Gaia might call in the mysterious boyfriend her foster mother had mentioned on the phone. Sam could take being one of Gaia's gang. He didn't think he could stand to see her cuddling with another guy.

A voice called from somewhere in another room. "Gaia? Aren't you going to introduce me to your friend before we leave?"

An annoyed look crossed Gaia's face. She finished pulling on her coat and zipped it closed. "We have to go!" she shouted back. "If you want to meet him, you'll have to hurry."

A woman stepped around the corner into the front room. She was wearing a short teal skirt and a tight white top instead of an emerald dress. But there was no mistaking the legs, the face, or the body. It was the same woman that Sam had met at the bar. The woman he had sex with only hours before.

Gaia gave a sigh. She waved a hand at the approaching woman. "Sam, this is Ella Niven."

The woman walked up slowly, a Cheshire grin on her hungry red mouth. She reached out a hand with nails lacquered to the exact shade of her lips. "Hello, Sam. I'm Gaia's foster mother."

Sam wished that fainting were still in fashion. Falling into darkness and having everything just go away sounded like a wonderful idea. Instead his brain seemed to separate from his body and float up to the high ceiling of the room. He saw his self standing there. The body's mouth was open in a stupid expression. Its eyes were wide and glassy.

Sam watched as Gaia stepped around in front of

166

the body. He saw the woman—Ella—looking at the body with an amazing expression that mingled amusement, playfulness, and a promise that another night might be waiting.

Gaia looked worried. "Sam? You okay?"

The body took a step back. The mouth closed, opened, closed.

From his perch up by the ceiling, Sam thought the body was about the funniest thing he had ever seen. He would have laughed if he still had a mouth to laugh with. It was nice and warm up near the ceiling. He felt fine there. It was good to be free of the body and all the stupid, embarrassing things that it could do.

"Sam?"

The body turned and stumbled to the front door.

Gaia moved after it. "Sam? Where are you going? What's wrong?"

The body made some meaningless sounds. It fumbled at the door, opened it, and fell out into the night.

At once the feeling of floating by the ceiling vanished. Sam was back inside his own skull as he ran down the sidewalk, pushing past people on their way to parties and celebrations. He could feel the cold wind chapping his cheeks and nose. He could feel the freezing tears that streamed from his eyes. He could feel the crushing weight of emotion that squeezed at his chest.

There was no escaping himself. No escaping the awful wreck he had made of his life.

GO AFTER HIM. YOU COULD catch him.

It was true enough. The same thing that made Gaia strong also made her fast. The visit to St. Mark's Place hadn't even been enough to

Nothing but a Tramp

dent the energy in Gaia's legs. She could run down Sam in half a block. But she wasn't sure what to do if she caught him. She had no idea what had made him run in the first place.

"I wonder what upset your friend," said Ella.

Gaia spun around and looked into her foster mother's face. As usual, there was a faint trace of a smile on Ella's lips. Except when she was angry, Ella always seemed to find everyone else in the world quite amusing.

"What do you know about it?" asked Gaia.

"Me?" Ella shook her head. "Why should I know anything?"

Gaia narrowed her eyes. "I don't know, but you do."

"Please. How should I know anything about this boy of yours?"

Gaia didn't bother to answer. Gaia was smart, but it didn't take a genius to know that Ella was hiding something. Somehow Ella knew something about Sam. And from Sam's reaction, Sam certainly thought he knew something about Ella.

"Where did you meet Sam?"

"Why, I'm not sure that I ever have," said Ella. "I'm not in the habit of associating with boys that young."

Gaia gritted her teeth. Ella might be in her thirties, but she certainly dressed like she still thought she was a teenager. Gaia knew that Ella was going out almost every night that George wasn't home—and sometimes even when he was. Ella wasn't fooling anybody but George. For some reason, George seemed completely blind to the things his much younger wife was doing. He was the only one who didn't realize Ella was nothing but a tramp.

If Ella was cheating on George, who was to say she was actually cheating with people her own age? Ella liked to dress younger. Maybe she liked to date younger, too. Maybe she was spending her nights running around with younger guys. Guys like Sam.

Gaia decided not to think about it. She turned and ran out the door.

THE UNITED NATIONS BUILDING

gleamed in the darkness. Tom Moore walked slowly along the curving rows of flags and hunched his shoulders against the cold wind, sending a ripple of pain through his rib cage. *I shouldn't be out here on a night like this,* he thought. *Not in this condition.*

Out of the Darkness

The snow that had started at sunset was falling more thickly as the night wore on. It whipped in between the multicolored banners and drifted up against the curb.

By the time Tom reached the meeting point, the snow had already covered the sidewalks. And was beginning to spread into the streets.

A figure came out of the darkness. Tom tensed for a moment, but as the man came closer he relaxed. Tom put out his hand. "It's good to see you."

George Niven gripped Tom's hand tightly. "It's been too long. Way too long." He looked back over his shoulder. "We better walk."

The two men turned and walked side by side along the icy sidewalk. "This is risky, George," Tom said. "You could have been followed."

"I spent the last hour making sure that I wasn't," George replied. "But don't worry. I don't intend to make this a regular event. I heard about what happened at your apartment. You look terrible."

"I'm fine." Tom glanced at the older agent, dismissing the subject. "So why are we out here in the snow? Have you seen Loki?"

"No. I have no doubt he's nearby, but I don't know where."

"Then why—"

"I think Gaia's in serious danger." George shoved his hands deep into the pockets of his coat and stared up at the fluttering flags.

"How do you know?" Tom asked.

George nodded. "I found a hidden microphone on one of her jackets." He lowered his eyes and looked at Tom. "I'd picked the jacket up off the banister, and as I was carrying it up to her room, I felt something prick my finger. I have no idea how it got there, but . . ."

"But it's got to be a Loki job," Tom finished.

George waved a hand through the air. "I'm almost positive." He paused and stared off into the darkness. "I have someone checking the device to see if we can trace it. Someone from the agency. But I'm not optimistic."

The implications of what George was saying swirled through Tom's mind. If Loki had been close enough to Gaia to have her bugged, then Gaia was under even closer observation than Tom had thought. Loki knew when she was home and when she was away. He knew everything, from what kind of music she was listening to what she ate for breakfast.

"You're right," said Tom. "My daughter is in even more danger than I knew."

George drew in a deep breath. "What do we do now, Tom?"

"I'd love to say that I'll come and get my daughter tonight," said Tom. "But I can't. Not in the shape I'm in. And not while we don't know what Loki's next move will be."

"So we keep waiting."

Tom nodded. "And when we get our chance, we act."

George walked over to the nearest flagpole and leaned against the metal base. "You mean we kill him."

"Yes. We'll do whatever we have to."

Tom pulled a gun from his pocket and studied it briefly before returning it to his coat. Then he shook George's hand again, turned, and walked away.

THE WEATHER HAD CUT DOWN ON

the crowds, but there were still at least a hundred people milling around near the arch at the center of Washington Square Park. Gaia stood

Innocent Explanations

on her tiptoes, looking for Mary—and hoping that she might see Sam—but neither one was among the crowd. Finally Gaia spotted Ed on the far side of the mass of people and hurried over to join him.

Ed was moving back and forth over the same patch of sidewalk. From the deep groves in the snow, it looked like he had been pacing for some time. He spotted Gaia as she approached and stopped. "Hey, I thought you were bringing Sam with you."

"I was." She shrugged and raised her gloved hands. "He weirded out on me." She started to say something about Ella but stopped herself. She didn't even want to think about it herself, much less give Ed a reason to start making theories. "I guess he's not coming."

Ed grunted. "I guess we're even, then. Mary never showed up."

"Maybe she's still waiting at her place."

"Tried it," Ed replied with a shake of his head. "I've called over there twice. No answer. Did you find our pal Mr. Skizz?"

Gaia nodded. "I found him, but I don't think he's the one after Mary." Thinking of Skizz's battered face, Gaia thought that looking in the mirror must be the scariest thing he did all day.

"Then where is she?"

Gaia wished she knew the answer. There could be a hundred innocent explanations. Mary was never the world's most organized person. She might

173

have gotten the time wrong or run off to do some other errand before they got together. Somehow Gaia didn't think so.

"Come on," she said. "We've got to go."

"Where?" asked Ed.

Gaia started walking. "We'll figure that out on the way."

MARY LEANED BACK INTO THE PLUSH

leather seat. "For a government guy, you've got a great car."

Loki laughed. It was a good laugh. Deep and reassuring. "Thanks. It comes with this assignment."

"Nice work if you can get it." The pain in Mary's leg was beginning to ease. After the terror of escaping the apartment and the

freezing air outside, it was great to feel safe and warm. She closed her eyes and listened to the soft hum of the car's big engine. She wondered if it would be too rude if she fell asleep on the way to the police station.

Loki took a right-hand turn at the next intersection. "What do you think they wanted?" he asked.

"Who?"

"Those people who tried to kill you."

"Oh, them." Mary had been so caught up in what the intruder in her apartment had been trying to do that she hadn't put much thought into who or why. The idea that someone was trying to kill her sort of shoved out all the other thoughts. Now that she was thinking about it, she found it was a pretty tough question.

There were a couple of obvious candidates. After all, Mary had been a very popular girl lately when it came to creeps and thugs.

The intruder could have been Skizz. Mary still owed him five hundred dollars for drugs she had taken before Gaia inspired her to drop the coke habit. Only Skizz wasn't exactly the type to bug someone's phone. He would never have been snooping around her apartment in the first place. He might kill her, sure, but the other stuff was too weird to be Skizz.

Mary also gave some thought to the sex-for-points bozos she had caught at the Village School. Two assholes from the gang had already tried to rape her. Now that Mary had helped to expose the ring, she was sure that they would love to get back at her. Except this thing with the case and the electronics wasn't exactly the kind of stunt that a bunch of dumb high school jocks would pull.

"I don't know," she confessed. "It's not like my family's rich or anything. I can't imagine what . . ." Mary stopped. Maybe she *could* imagine. A memory drifted through her head: Aunt Jen on a crackling phone line.

"Did you think of something?" asked the government man.

Mary nodded. "Maybe. It might have something to do with this friend of mine. A girl named Gaia Moore."

"Gaia?" The man slowed the car and glanced over at Mary. "I know Gaia."

"You do?"

"More than know her. She's my niece."

Mary stared at the man behind the wheel. "You're Gaia Moore's uncle?" The idea excited her so much that she nearly forgot the pain in her leg. It was almost too good to be true. In fact, it almost seemed like it *couldn't* be true. She shot the man a doubtful glance. "Man, what are the odds?"

"Actually, it's not all that coincidental," Loki answered. "I came into town especially to check on Gaia. And her foster parents said she might be with you." The man cast another glance at Mary. There was a tense expression on his face. "So what makes you think that these people who were in your apartment have anything to do with my niece?"

Mary started to blurt out a response but realized

there were things she probably shouldn't say in front of Gaia's uncle. "Gaia told me something," she said carefully. "Something about her mom."

The man sighed. "Katia. Gaia told you about how she died." He steered the car through another right turn.

"Yeah."

"And did you share that information with anyone else?"

A twinge of pain ran up Mary's leg. She twisted in her seat. "I told part of it to my aunt Jen. She works at the library. I thought she might be able to find out something that would help Gaia."

"Your aunt. Yes." Loki looked at her with a strange intensity. "Anyone else?"

"No." Mary peeked out her window. It seemed like they had been driving for a long time. "Are we almost at the police station?"

"Soon," said Loki. "You're sure you didn't tell anyone but your aunt?"

Mary nodded. "Only Aunt Jen." A medium-sized apartment building swung into view through curtains of blowing snow. "Hey!"

"What's wrong?" asked Loki.

"That's my building." Mary ignored fresh pain from her leg and brought her face close to the foggy side window. "We've been going around in circles."

"We have?" Loki pulled around a double-parked minivan. "I must have taken a wrong turn."

A tightness began to slowly squeeze

Mary's throat. "What police station were you going to, anyway?"

"Actually," Loki replied, "I thought we should do something about your injuries before we went to the authorities."

"Are we going to a hospital?" asked Mary.

"Not necessary." Loki abruptly stopped the car in the middle of the street. He twisted and reached into the car's backseat.

Mary leaned away from him. "What are you doing?"

Loki pulled back a case. A small, leather case, sort of like the one Mary used to carry her flute in for band. Deftly Loki popped the catches at the side of the case and flipped it open.

"I have just the thing for your pain," he said.

Loki reached into the case, pulled out a vial of cocaine, and threw it to Mary.

ED'S ARMS HAD BEEN DOING LEG

duty for over a year, but he couldn't remember his shoulders ever being so tired. "Where are we going now?"

Deep Breaths

Gaia Moore marched ahead of him, her torn

sneakers crunching through the snow. "Back to the brownstone."

Ed groaned. "You can't mean your brownstone."

Gaia nodded without turning. "The one where I stay, yeah."

"But we've already been there," Ed replied. "And we've been to Mary's apartment, and back to the club, and to half a dozen local restaurants and made at least that many trips across the park."

Gaia stopped in her tracks. She didn't say anything at first, but Ed could see her back moving in and out as she took deep, deep breaths.

Somehow I don't think this is going to be good, Ed thought.

"We're going back because Mary might be there," said Gaia.

"I understand, but—"

Gaia spun around and stomped back to Ed. "What's your idea, huh? Where do you think she is?"

"I don't—"

"Because you know what I think?" said Gaia. "I think she's in trouble!" She leaned over Ed and slammed her hands down on the arms of his wheelchair. "I knew she was in trouble, but I didn't help her."

"You tried to," said Ed. He looked up at Gaia and shivered. There was enough tension in her to light half the city. "Look, I'm sure Mary's okay."

179

Gaia let out a breath that whistled through her teeth. "How the hell can you know that?"

MARY LOOKED THROUGH THE CURVING
side of the small glass vial. The powder inside was so white, so fine.

Loyalty

"Go ahead," said Loki. "You want it, don't you?"

Mary wanted to say no, but instead she nodded. "Yes," she said in a harsh, breathy voice.

She reached over and took the vial from his hands. She did want it. Mary wanted the rush, but more than that she wanted the energy and the feeling of being able to think so much better. "You're not really Gaia's uncle, are you?"

"I am." Loki started the car moving again and took a hard left. "Now, take your medicine like a good girl."

Electric wires. Mary felt like all her nerves had been replaced with tight, hot electric wires. She wanted the cocaine. She needed it.

Mary ran her finger along the black plastic top of the vial. A few loose grains of powder stuck to her fingers. Want it. Need it.

"Take it," repeated Loki. "The sooner you're done, the sooner you can see Gaia."

Gaia.

Mary ran her finger over the glass one last time. Then she dropped the vial on the floorboard of the sedan, raised her foot, and crushed the little bottle under her heel.

"I promised I would stay straight." Mary ground the cocaine into the sedan's dark carpet.

"Promises are very important," said Loki. And then he swung his arm in a lightning-fast back-handed slap that drove his knuckles into Mary's mouth.

The blow was like an explosion. Mary's head snapped back. Incredible pain lanced through her mouth.

"Now," said Loki. His voice was flat calm. "Let's go over a few things again. Did you tell anyone?"

Mary raised a trembling hand to her mouth. Her fingers came back covered in blood.

"Did you tell anyone?" said Loki.

He didn't raise his voice, but his tone left no doubt he expected an answer.

"No," Mary mumbled through her torn lips. "Nobody."

The second blow was blindingly fast.

Mary's head went back so hard, sparks ran across her vision.

"I already know you told your aunt," said Loki. "Isn't that right?"

"Yes," Mary cried. "Yes."

Loki nodded. "So you did tell someone," he said as

he turned the car around another corner. "And did you tell anyone else?"

"No."

"You're certain."

Mary nodded. "Yes." She sniffed. "Don't you know that already?"

"If you're referring to the devices I left at your home?" Loki shrugged. "Unfortunately, they don't always pick up everything."

"There was no one else."

Loki nodded. "For the sake of both you and Gaia, let's hope you're telling the truth."

LOKI STEERED THE BLACK SEDAN

around the corner. "Don't worry," he said. "We'll be getting out soon."

Mary sagged against the window. "And then what?"

Loki didn't answer. Instead he pulled the car over to the side of the road and parked. He left the engine at a low, smooth rumble. The windshield wipers continued to drive back and forth, clearing the heavy, wet flakes of snow.

It was time to end the threat posed by Mary Moss. Loki intended to not only ensure that the girl would never share what she had learned about Katia's death but also to put an end to Gaia's experiment in friendship. When this was over, Gaia would never again dare to share her deepest feelings with anyone—except, of course, her dear uncle.

Loki reached into his pocket and pulled out a black stocking cap. "It's time to get out."

The girl looked at him suspiciously. "I don't suppose that means you're letting me go?"

Loki had no intention of letting Mary go free, but he knew well enough how a little hope could make it easier to keep a prisoner under control. "Come with me and answer a few questions. Then you're free to do as you please."

The expression on the girl's face was one of mingled fear, doubt, and hope. It was clear to Loki that she didn't really believe him, but it was just as clear that she desperately *wanted* to believe. "I thought you were going to kill me."

"Answer my questions, and I'll have no reason to kill you." He pulled the black mask over his face and got out of the car.

The heavy blanket of snow softened his footsteps as he circled the car. Loki checked the area to be sure that no observer was too close before opening the door. There was no one. He jerked open the door, letting in a swirl of snow.

The girl tumbled out and tried to stand. Loki looked down at her.

"Don't try to run," he said. He raised one side of his coat and revealed a heavy black pistol attached to a long tube.

"Silencer," mumbled Mary. "That's what the other thing was in the case."

"Come with me," said Loki. "I'd prefer not to use this if I don't have to."

Mary nodded. She began walking along the sidewalk in slow, small steps. Her feet slipped frequently in the snow.

Loki stayed close. "That's good," he said. "Keep moving."

Mary stopped and shook her head. "No," she said softly.

Loki was on her in one quick stride. He grabbed the front of her coat and pulled Mary toward him. "I said I would prefer not to use the gun. I didn't say I would hesitate."

"Are you really Gaia's uncle?" the girl asked.

"Yes." There was no harm in telling her anything now. The girl would never have the chance to spread her information.

"And after you kill me, what are you going to do to Gaia?"

Loki gave a tug on her coat. "I've already told you. Talk and you're in no further danger."

The girl gave a weak nod. She started to move again, but two steps down the sidewalk her knees folded, and she collapsed in the snow.

Loki took her by the arm and lifted her. Mary dangled from Loki's hand like a doll.

He gritted his teeth. "Get up." Mary continued to hang limply from his hand. Loki removed the silencer and put it back into his pocket. He took the dark, heavy bulk of the Glock pistol and pressed the blunt barrel against Mary's back. "Answer my questions, and I'll set you free. Stay here and die."

Mary got her feet back under her and stood. She trembled in Loki's grip, but when he gave her a nudge with the gun, she began to walk.

Loki steered his captive along. "Her death was an accident."

Even in the dim light he could see the girl's eyes grow wide. "You killed her?"

"I loved her," said Loki.

He jerked on Mary's arm. They were in the midst of a small grove. Ordinarily they might have been visible from half the park, but the driving sheets of snow closed in around them like walls. Everything more than a dozen yards away was lost in curtains of white.

"Stop here," said Loki. He released his grip on her. "Turn around and face me."

Mary slowly spun around. "You killed Gaia's mother."

Loki put his gloved hand in the girl's hair and shoved back her head. "It was an accident."

185

"Right, I believe you." Despite her awkward position Mary suddenly smiled. "So, who were you trying to kill?"

Loki took the Glock pistol and leveled it at Mary's forehead. "Gaia's father." His finger slipped inside the trigger guard.

He barely noticed the girl's right hand coming up. It wasn't until her hand was in front of his eyes that Loki realized he had been careless.

And then his face exploded in pain.

GAIA HAD READ THAT SOME BLIND

people developed a better sense of hearing. Or sense of smell. Or touch.

Maybe it was true; maybe it was nothing more than another urban legend. All Gaia knew was that she couldn't feel fear, but she could feel everything else. Sometimes she wondered if she felt them more than normal, frightened people.

At the moment what she felt was rage. Rage and frustration.

You should know better than to think you're normal. You should know better than to think you can have friends. You should know better than to think you might possibly, one day, be happy.

Ed rolled up beside her. His breath steamed in the light of the nearest streetlamp. "If this snow gets any deeper, I won't be able to move."

Gaia kicked at the path. Six inches of snow and it was still falling. The weather would pick tonight for a decent snow. "It doesn't matter," she said. "I don't know where to go."

"What about the park?" suggested Ed.

Gaia glanced at him. "Why?"

Ed spun his chair around and pointed back the way they had come. "That's where we said we'd meet her. If she's looking for us, that's probably where she'll go."

"I thought you were too tired to move."

"Not yet." Ed gave her a tired grin. "But if it keeps snowing, you might have to carry me home."

MARY RAN UNDER THE THIN, BARE

Mummy

branches of the winter trees. She had lost the path. The snow covered everything, obscuring the boundaries between path and field and playground. Everything looked the same. Black trees. White snow.

She struggled along on her injured leg. At every step it seemed that her foot got heavier. After a hundred yards she was limping. After two hundred she dragged the leg behind her, leaving long cuts in the snow like some mummy from an old movie limping across the sand.

"Help!" she shouted, but it seemed that the snow muffled her voice. "Gaia!"

The snow was falling faster than ever. It made it hard to see more than a few feet ahead. Mary knew that she was still in the park, but she didn't know where.

She might be near the chessboards or the fountain. The Arc de Triomphe might be no more than a dozen yards away, cloaked by night and snow.

"Gaia!"

The same thought ran through her head over and over. *I have to find Gaia. I have to warn her about her uncle.*

HALFWAY TO THE PARK GAIA GOT

behind Ed and pushed. Even with her help, getting the chair through the deepening snow was a struggle. It was **Fireworks** ridiculous to even try it. The only thing that made sense was to help Ed get home.

But inside, something seemed to hammer at her. Hurry. Hurry.

No more than two dozen people were waiting near the arch by the time they reached the center of the park. None of them looked anything like Mary Moss.

"How long do we wait?" asked Ed.

Gaia shook her head. She was all out of answers. *I have to find Mary.*

"Gaia."

The call was so faint that at first Gaia was sure she had imagined it. Then it came again.

"Gaia."

"Did you hear that?" asked Gaia.

Ed raised his head. "Hear what?"

Before Gaia could reply, the fireworks finally started. Sparkles of gold and silver mixed with and lit the falling snow.

Gaia didn't stop to watch. She turned and ran into the night.

BLOOD WAS FROZEN ON MARY'S

Close

cheek. She could barely breathe. Her eyes teared in the bitter cold. Her leg ached from hip to ankle.

When the colors started in the sky, she

189

thought it was an illusion. It was only after the second explosion and the third that she realized it was the fireworks at the center of the park.

Gaia was close. All she had to do was follow the fireworks.

"Gaia!" she shouted again.

She limped forward a step. Another step.

A tall, dark figure appeared from behind a tree. "I have to give you credit," said Loki. "You came very close." He raised the gun over his head and brought the handle of the heavy weapon down in a vicious blow.

This time the fireworks were all inside Mary's head.

LOKI'S EYES WERE STILL STREAMING

with tears. He risked removing his **mask** for a moment, bent, grabbed a handful of snow, and rubbed it across his burning face. Then he carefully replaced his mask. Even with the heavy snow, the park wasn't completely empty. If he were seen, the situation would be severely complicated.

Blunt Instrument

Despite the pain her attack had caused, Loki felt

even more regret about killing the girl. Mary Moss had proved to be quite resourceful. It was true that she had become too close to Gaia, but if Mary could be turned, that closeness could become an advantage. Mary might be used to manipulate Gaia in ways that a blunt instrument like Ella could never achieve.

No. She knows about Katia. She can't be allowed to survive.

Mary groaned and rolled over in the snow. Her eyes blinked open. "Gaia," she groaned.

Before she could do anything more, Loki drove the toe of his boot into her side. The girl let out a little yip. A small hand with bright red nails reached toward his ankle. Loki stomped down hard on the pale fingers, then sent another kick into the girl's body.

This time he was rewarded by a low, whistling moan before his victim passed out. Mary Moss would be giving him no more trouble.

Loki once again put his fingers in the girl's red hair. He pulled her unconscious form to her knees, moved around behind her, and put the Glock at the base of her skull. It would look like a drug hit. That's what the girl's parents would think. That's what the police would think. Most important, that's what Gaia would think.

And Gaia would learn a very important lesson— don't get too close. Otherwise you might get hurt.

Loki put his finger on the trigger.

"No!" came a scream from his left.

Loki felt a sense of movement. The sense of something rushing toward him out of the darkness and snow.

He pulled the trigger.

GAIA COLLIDED WITH THE MAN JUST
as the gun exploded. For the tiniest slice of a second the muzzle flash lit the snow around her, freezing the motion of every snowflake like the world's loudest strobe light.

Frozen Moment

In that moment of light Gaia could see everything. She could see the wool knit of the man's mask. She could see the black pistol in his gloved hand. She could see the bruises on Mary's face, and the blood on her split lips, and how her ginger hair was blown aside by the bullet on its way to her brain.

The frozen moment ended. Gaia's momentum knocked the man from his feet and sent him sprawling in the snow. Gaia didn't go down. She landed on her feet, skidded, and jumped again to find the man already getting up.

Gaia put a sneaker in his hidden face. The man sat back down in the snow. Gaia launched another kick.

When fighting, Gaia usually worked hard not to cause permanent damage. This wasn't usually. She aimed her blow at the man's neck and delivered it with enough force to send his head bouncing all the way to Eighth Street.

The man blocked. It was a fast, efficient flip of his left arm, just enough to send Gaia's foot grazing past its target.

The missed kick sent Gaia flying over him. She tucked down her head, did a quick tumble, and rolled back to her feet. By the time she turned around, the man was also standing.

Gaia circled left, faked right, and went in. She sent a stiff right hand aiming for his face. Blocked. A spin kick at his side. Blocked. A sharp uppercut at his chin. Blocked.

She took a step back and studied the man. He held his hands low, almost too low, but he was fast. Gaia gritted her teeth. He wasn't fast enough. No one was.

Gaia went back another step, then came forward in an electric rush. She flew into the air with her stiff right leg aimed at the man's head.

The man raised an arm to block, but Gaia adjusted her aim midflight. She lowered her foot and drove it square in the center of the man's chest. He staggered back, but before Gaia could follow up her attack, she was forced to duck a whistling right hand that shattered the air only inches from her face.

This guy was good. Most of the idiots Gaia fought were completely clueless. Some of them had packed on a lot of prison muscle, and they probably looked pretty tough. Gaia wasn't impressed by looks. Even the tough guys were slow and easy. Not this guy. He was big and fast. More than that—he was trained.

The man feinted a kick, then withdrew another step.

Gaia followed. She threw a punch. Blocked. Kick. Blocked. Punch. A solid blow to the man's gut. Kick. A glancing shot to his hip but still enough to make him take another clumsy step. Leg sweep. The man in the black ski mask went down.

Gaia took her time. One more shot. That was all it would take. When it came right down to it, people were so easy to kill.

There was movement on her left. Gaia whipped around to face this new attack.

It was Mary. Her outstretched right hand clawed at the snow.

The man in the mask hadn't managed to touch Gaia a single time, but one look at Mary hit her like a bus. Gaia took a step toward her fallen friend. Then she remembered the man in the mask. Gaia turned back to face her enemy.

He was gone.

194

Gaia hurried forward. There were footsteps in the deepening snow. If she followed, she could catch the man. She was sure of it. All she had to do was leave Mary.

That was not an option.

She ran back to where Mary lay. Blood was spreading in the snow. It was splashed around Mary and speckled for a dozen yards in all directions. Mary's hand had stopped its fitful clawing at the earth. Mary's legs were still.

Images flashed through Gaia's mind. A house in the snow. Her mother. Blood and snow. Over and over, blood and snow. Gaia moved toward Mary as if she was wading through all her worst nightmares.

She's dead. She had to be dead. There was so much blood.

Gaia knelt in the stained snow. Tears made her vision waver, and her hands trembled as she reached out to touch Mary's cheek. Above her, shifting, sparking colors appeared as a fresh round of fireworks burst over the park. "Mary?"

To Gaia's astonishment, Mary's eyes opened. Her face was a mask of blood and pain, but her eyes immediately locked on Gaia's face. "Gaia?" she said in a weak, weirdly distorted voice.

"It's me." Gaia ran a hand over her friend's hair. Her fingers came back warm and sticky with blood. "Don't worry. You're going . . . You'll be okay."

Mary gave a single slow nod. "Gaia."

Gaia leaned in close. "Yeah."

"I was so worried about you," said Mary. Then her eyes slid back, and a final shiver ran through her body.

Gaia threw back her head and screamed into the falling snow.

LOKI STOOD BACK AMONG THE TREES

and watched as Gaia knelt over the fallen girl. He felt a moment of fear when he realized that the Moss girl was still alive, but then he saw the final shudder rack her body and knew that the threat was finally over.

Crimson Halo

"Where are you!" Gaia screamed at the night. "Where are you, you bastard!"

Loki didn't move. He didn't dare move. There were sharp pains in his hip and chest. He was quite certain that at least one of his ribs was broken. If Gaia found him, he had no doubt the girl would leave him as dead as he had left Mary Moss.

For an uncomfortable moment it seemed like Gaia was peering straight at Loki's hiding place. Then she turned and ran back toward the people at the center of the park.

Loki waited until Gaia was out of sight, then he went back to Mary. He took two glassine envelopes of cocaine from his pocket and slipped them into the dead girl's coat. Then he opened a third envelope and poured a bit of the powder across her frozen face.

He took one last look to satisfy himself that everything was as it should be, then he started out of the park. For the police everything would be neat and easy. Junkie girl dies. Drugs on the body. Even if they never found someone to blame, they would never look very hard for an answer.

As Loki reached the sedan and climbed inside, he wondered how Gaia would react. The situation of the death—the death, the gunshot, the blood—it was bound to conjure images of her mother. Its effect on Gaia should be interesting.

Loki pressed the speakerphone button on the car's dash. "The task is completed," he said. He reached for the button to hang up the phone, then paused. "Have someone standing by to clean up the car," he said. "There's blood on my upholstery."

He hung up the phone and drove away.

…[illegible] …would smell. Gus was out of sight until he
was back in Mary. He parked… as inconspicuous a
place as… into his pocket and slipped them into that
dead guy's coat. Then he wiped a tinfoil… [illegible]
portable tank the power… [illegible] frozen and…

He took another look to satisfy himself that everything was sure should be. He straightened out as the
guy… For the police to… [illegible] would be the usual
say, "Drunk or retarded… Drug… or Nobody. Even
if they never found an answer to… [illegible] …would
never bother… hard for answers.

He took the… lamp and placed inside the
wound of… Gus would read. The situation of the
death—the double… question, the how—it was
insane to… [illegible] image of… [illegible] to get him
too. He… be… [illegible]

Off pressed the… [illegible] button on the rig…
keys. The… complete… he said. He reached for
a… switch… letting go the phone then gunned… [illegible]
smelled… or so shut up etc. can," he said.
"Thanks… or my apology."…

…rising up the phone and drive away.

here is a
sneak peek of
Fearless™ #9:
BLOOD

So I've been trying to come up
with a snappy reply to all the
"I'm so sorry's" I've been getting about Mary. Yesterday at
school was pretty bad. Most of
those people didn't even know
Mary, except from seeing her at
parties. They didn't know her favorite band (Fearless), her
favorite color (fuschia), her
favorite food (satay). So why are
they all giving me these lame
expressions of grief? All yesterday,
during class, after class, I felt
their eyes boring holes into me—
which, frankly, was the last
thing I needed.

If it weren't for the fact
that I have gone through worse,
I would say that I couldn't bear
it. But of course, I can. And I
will. I am my father's daughter.
Just like him, I'm better off on
my own. I should know better
than to ever think that will
change.

I am the invincible, genetic
freak Gaia.

I just thank God Mary didn't
go to this school—it would have
made it all a hundred times
worse. Thanks, Mary.

If only she knew
where he hid
during the
day, like vermin.
Then she
could simply **never**
arrive, **again**
announce a
Candygram, and
take him apart.

ED SHOVELED A SMALL FORKFUL OF

chicken potpie into his mouth.
He glanced across the school
cafeteria table at Gaia. Day two
after Mary's death and Gaia was
still showing no signs of
weakness.

What's a chicken pot?

"What is chicken potpie, anyway?" Ed asked. "What's a
chicken pot? Like a pot just to
make chicken in? Where do they
get these names?"

Gaia looked up at him and almost smiled. That is,
her lips pressed together in a flat line for a moment.
Which was the most he'd gotten out of her in two
days.

She shrugged. "It's hot. You didn't have to make it.
What's the problem?" She took a bite of her own lunch.

Ed stared back down at the table, defeated. Then
he glanced back at Gaia. "You know, I'm glad you're
not a vegetarian," he said, desperate to make conversation. "I don't get the whole vegetarian thing. I mean, if
we're not supposed to eat animals, why are they made
out of meat?"

Not an original line, but Ed had forgotten what co-
median had said it first. Still, even though it was the
Ed Fargo Entertainment hour, he was not getting any reaction.

204

He tried again. "Why don't we go see a movie? Get your mind off of stuff."

Gaia met his eyes. Clear blue eyes, as untroubled as a spring morning in Maine. "No thanks," she said. "I've got some stuff to do at home."

Ed's eyes narrowed. Their mutual good friend had been shot and killed three days ago, and Gaia hadn't cried on his shoulder, hadn't expressed regret, hadn't mentioned Mary's name. Gaia had actually been holding Mary when she died. Now it was like Mary had never existed. And like Ed didn't exist, either.

In the four months he had known Gaia, Ed had seen her furious, violent, shy, antisocial, rude, sensitive, generous, forgiving, and reckless. He didn't think he had ever seen her truly happy, and he knew he had never seen her weak—either physically or emotionally. Why was he expecting something different now, just because her other best friend had been gunned down in front of her only two days ago?

Abruptly Ed pushed his lunch tray away. Suddenly, he didn't feel like eating anymore. What was this "stuff to do at home" shit? Gaia didn't consider the Nivens' house her *home*. He leaned across the table, his eyes narrowing. "Who are you, and what have you done with the real Gaia?"

It was an old joke, an ancient joke, but still chuckle-worthy, in Ed's opinion. *Could we at least see a glimmer of a smile, please?*

Instead, Gaia looked suddenly inexpressibly sad. It was only for a moment, but a shadow passed over Gaia's features. Then it was gone. Her face twitched back into its beautiful, expressionless mask. "There is no real Gaia," she said softly.

SLITHER. CROSS. SLITHER. ELLA loved the sound her thigh-high stockings made when she crossed and uncrossed her legs. Sort **So powerful** of slippery and smooth at the same time.

"Go on." Loki turned to face her, his back against the anonymous white wall of this apartment. At first Ella had been surprised that Loki had chosen a doorman building for this month's pied-à-terre. Then she realized that the heavy-jowled gorilla in the cheesy maroon uniform was no doubt on Loki's payroll.

Ella shrugged, crossed her legs again, and felt a wave of pleasure and irritation tingling at the base of her spine. "What can I tell you? You offed her friend, right in front of her. But she hasn't been crying, hasn't been doing anything. As a matter of fact," Ella said thoughtfully, examining a one-inch-long spiky fingernail, "she's been slightly less unbearable lately. At least she's coming home for meals and not sneaking out at night. So George isn't quite as worried about her as he usually is."

The force of Loki's intense gaze made Ella's cheeks burn. Damn him. Even after years he could do this to her. She thought about what Loki was like in bed. Blurred images flitted through her mind, Loki sliding next to her, the cord in his neck tightening as he moved. She visualized his almost surgical precision, an almost superhuman control. Loki was so dangerous, so frightening, so powerful. Falling for him had been as intense and as addicting as jumping off a cliff. But for now, Ella had to focus on business.

"Has she been with her other friends?" he asked. "The wheelchair guy? Ed? Anyone from school? Anyone . . . else?"

Like Sam Moon, you mean? Ella thought sarcastically. She had to gulp hard to keep a grin off her face. Sam Moon had been *delicious.* Absolutely delicious. Ladies, you don't need Prozac: you need a young, unstoppable, pretty boy to put the smiles back on your faces. Not only had Sam been fabulous in bed—strong, uncomplicated, and enthusiastic—but there had been an added layer of pleasure in knowing that Ella was sleeping with the object of Gaia's affection. She almost laughed out loud just thinking about it. Gaia, that perverse, hateful, genetic freak, was eating her guts out over Sam Moon. And Ella had bagged him before Gaia did. It was almost too perfect.

"Ella?" Loki demanded.

Ella snapped back to the present and shook her head. "No. Like I said, she's been staying home," Ella said. "Not making phone calls, not sneaking out. Yesterday she stopped for a slice of pizza on her way home from school, but that's hardly unusual. She has the undiscriminating taste of a hyena."

Loki regarded Ella coldly. "She's a survivor. Like a hyena, you could put her down almost anywhere, and she would survive. She would adapt. She is very strong, our Gaia."

A tiny muscle twitched in Ella's smoothly made-up cheek. God, she hated that bitch. To hear Loki salivating over her was nauseating.

"Uh-huh," Ella said, trying to keep the irritation out of her voice. She didn't quite succeed. Jesus, how long was this going to go on? She shivered without meaning to, just thinking of the weather outside. She wanted to be somewhere far away. Somewhere warm. But no, Ella was stuck here, playing baby-sitter to her foster daughter. Daughter. Ella swallowed hard.

LOKI TURNED HIS BACK TO ELLA AND

Worthy strode over to the windows. It was already dark, at four-thirty. From these windows he could see the big X formed by Broadway and Seventh Avenue as they crossed and reversed positions. He sighed. Ella was rapidly reaching the limits of her usefulness. The open hatred on her face when she spoke of Gaia was more than annoying. Still, he knew Ella was under control. She wouldn't dare touch a hair on that beautiful head.

Loki sighed again, this time with pleasure. In the window's reflection, he could see Ella, behind him, no longer even bothering to pretend to pay attention to him. She looked at her nails, crossed and uncrossed her legs, yawned, gazed at the ceiling. The fact that she failed to be inspired by Gaia was proof of her own inadequacy.

Gaia alone was perfect. Gaia alone was worthy—worthy of her background, her training, her surveillance. Worthy of his attention. Worthy of something more than attention. The fact that Gaia had witnessed the death of one of the pathetic props in her difficult life—had witnessed it and not crumpled, had watched her friend die and yet shown no signs of weakness or trivial human emotion in the days following—well, that just proved how very special his beloved niece was.

GAIA STEPPED OFF THE NUMBER

6 local on 96th Street and started walking west. The February cold whistled down the wind tunnels made by tall buildings on either side of her. It whipped her hair around beneath the sweat-

It's almost funny

shirt hood that stuck up from beneath her puffy blue ski jacket.

It hadn't been easy ditching Ed. First he'd asked her to a movie. Then after school he had suggested eating together or even—sacrifice of all sacrifices—going shopping.

She'd rejected him flat out. He'd sat, watching her, as she booked east to catch the green line. She hadn't looked back.

Now, reaching Fifth Avenue, Gaia turned left, then crossed the wide street, heading for the huge columns of the Metropolitan Museum of Art. Her plan was simple: first, an hour of culture, then a bowl of potato-leek soup from the soup Nazi, then a couple of hours in and around Thompkins Square Park, enjoying the lovely January weather and looking for her good old pal Skizz. Gaia shivered once, as if someone had just drawn long fingernails down a chalkboard. Skizz had *looked* pretty harmless after the last beating Gaia had given him.

But she had no doubt in her mind that he was the one who ordered the hit on Mary. One of his asshole dealer friends had probably owed him a favor. But Gaia wasn't fooled. She knew who was to blame. She'd been fooled once by Skizz, but never again.

If only she knew where he slept, where he ate, where he hid during the day like vermin. Then she could simply arrive, announce a Candygram, and take him apart. A couple times.

But Gaia was going to wait until the time was right. She would wait until well after night fell. Hence her quest for culture in the meantime.

When she walked through the huge, heavy bronze doors of the museum, a strong, heated blast of air whooshed down on her. It instantly dried the snowflakes clinging to her hair. Inside it was stuffy, overheated, and dry. Gaia shrugged out of the puffy ski jacket and tied its floppy arms around her waist. She snagged a map from the info desk and made her way to a bank of elevators.

An elevator, a couple of long halls, and a wide stairway later, Gaia found herself in a series of rooms devoted to German Expressionists. As Gaia wandered over in front of a Nolde painting, she had a flashback of her mother. Katia. Katia had taught Gaia how to look at art, how to love it, how to let it get inside her. Remembering those lessons, Gaia sank down on a bare wooden bench and stared at the painting in front of her.

The painting was called "Three Russians," and it showed two men and a woman all bundled up, as if, perhaps, they had just strolled down a New York street in the middle of January. The brushstrokes were coarse and broad; the paint clung thickly to the canvas in crusty swaths. Three Russians. All dressed in fur. They had long, thin noses, high cheekbones . . .

Katia Moore had been Russian. Gaia had hated her accent, had been embarrassed by her rolling r's, her formal hairstyle, the clothes she brought from Europe. She had been so unlike other kids' mothers. Gaia's whole family had been so unlike everyone else's. Which is why she was here, now, seventeen years old, a genetic freak made freakier by her father's intensive, relentless training. Training that had ended as abruptly as her mother's life, and on the same night.

Gaia's breath lightly left her lungs as she felt herself sink into the hard bench. It was so hot in here, so dry.

Why? she screamed silently. Why had she been made into such a freak? As a child, when she realized, when she *knew* that she simply never felt fear, it hadn't been a big deal. In fact, she hadn't really stuck out as a kid, except for her height. But lots of kids had seemed reckless and fearless—like that day she and four of her friends climbed up to the roof of the Rosenblitts' shed, jumped from there to the roof of the Stapletons' garage, then crossed over to the other side and leaped seven feet down onto a pile of compost. Paratroopers! Okay, it had been disgusting, landing in all the fruit rinds and eggshells, but it hadn't been scary. Not for any of them. It had been fun.

But now, at seventeen, never feeling fear had become a weight around her neck, relentlessly dragging her down. But then, her fearlessness was also a good thing, because it meant that nothing would stop Gaia from wiping Skizz out. Her intellect surely wasn't going to get in the way. Her emotions were on vacation. And she didn't feel fear. End result? No Skizz. No Skizz ever again. Just like no—

Gaia suddenly felt hungry. Maybe it was time to hit the soup wagon. She took one last quick look around at the German Expressionists. Gotta hand it to them—they were masters at expressing all the agonies of the human condition. Thwarted love, psychic torture, the sheer pain of existence all laid out for the viewer in bright jewellike colors. All these paintings of anguish. It was almost funny. Gaia hiked up her messenger bag, turned, and left the Three Russians behind.

Skizz is lying low. I almost froze my ass off last night in Thompkins Square Park, but after five hours, he hadn't shown his ugly face. But I'll get him. After I got back to George's last night I couldn't sleep. I thought about all the ways I could kill Skizz. Facing him, sideways, from the back. In my mind I heard his shoulder snap as I bent it. I heard the choked scream of pain rip from his throat as I broke his fingers, one by one.

The thing is, it won't be a lesson. Sometimes bullies need to be taught lessons, and if I'm around, I'm happy to do it. Call it my contribution to society. But the statute of limitations for Skizz to learn his lessons ran out a couple days ago. He's failed the exam. He gets no second chance.

He doesn't know it, but every hour he breathes is one less hour until his own personal doomsday. I promise you. I promise you.

She could
feel him
watching
her. It
didn't
matter. It
didn't
matter. It
didn't
matter.

**lower
than
low**

"I'LL GO WITH YOU."

Gaia's eyes narrowed as she looked at Ed. She leaned back enough to shut her locker door, then dropped her messenger bag to the floor so she could put on her ski jacket. A few

Not quite succeeding

limp, grayish feathers leaked out through the hole and fluttered to the ground. Ed watched them fall.

"No thanks," she said, trying not to sound regretful and not quite succeeding. "I think I'll just go do it. I need to get this paper done." Picking up her messenger bag, she slung it over her shoulder and jerked her hair out from beneath the strap.

Ed's wheelchair blocked her way. "What is *with* you?"

Forcing her face to remain calm, Gaia shrugged. She could see the frustration and uncertainty on his face, and for a moment she wished it weren't there.

"What do you mean?"

"The way you're acting." Ed's arms made choppy movements in the air as he struggled to express himself, obviously wary of how far to push her. "I mean, I'm trying to comfort you here, trying to be a good friend. This is a hard time for you—for me too. But you just keep acting like I should go screw myself."

216

"This isn't a hard time for me," Gaia said evenly. "And I'm not acting like you should go screw yourself. But I have this paper due. I'm tired of all the teachers giving me a hard time. I just want to do some stuff, get them off my back. I'm sorry if that's inconveniencing you."

Ed's eyes bored into hers. "Gaia . . ."

"Gotta go," Gaia said briskly. "Bye." She made a quick pivot around his wheelchair and strode toward the east side entrance of the school. The one with stairs. The one Ed couldn't follow her out of. She could feel him watching her. It didn't matter. It didn't matter. It didn't matter.

NOW, WHY DOESN'T STARBUCKS

The non—excited state

have a concession stand right here? Sam Moon wondered. He stretched and yawned, his heavy-weight sweater riding up to expose some smooth skin and a thin strip of stomach hair. What day was it? He looked at his watch. It gave him only a number. Ah! An abandoned newspaper lay crumpled in the deep armchair next to his. It was Thursday. Assuming that this was today's newspaper.

The life of the pre-med student. All work and no play. Actually, Sam's life often consisted of too much play and not enough work. His grades had demonstrated just that at the end of last semester. Which had prompted a heartfelt man-to-man with Dad, which had prompted Sam's working his butt off for the last six weeks. He looked around the study room he was in. The NYU library was ten stories tall, with a huge open vertical space in the middle, and floor after floor of books encircling it like a vise. It made him feel nauseated just looking at it.

But down here in one of the first-floor study rooms, he could block out the rest of the cavernous building and experience only the hushed quiet of the room, the sound-deadening camel-colored carpet, the deeply ugly tweed-covered easy chairs that dotted the room like chicken pox on a first-grader.

Sam shifted again in his seat, feeling his muscles' achy protest. How long had he been sitting here, wading through the text and class notes for his human sexuality class? At least three hours, with only one bathroom break. He needed coffee. He needed a Danish or something. At the beginning of the year, someone had turned him on to onion bagels with scallion cream cheese. He'd thought they were incredible, until the night he'd thrown one up through his nose after a bout of tequila shots in Josh Seidman's dorm room.

Once you throw something up through your nose, you never want to eat it again. Fact of life.

Human sexuality. What a laugh. The course was required for pre-meds, and he and his pals thought it would be a hoot. Instead, it somehow managed to suck every last bit of titillating humor from the subject, and turn it into something so dry that sometimes Sam wondered if the team who wrote the textbook had ever, ever gotten it on *once* in their whole dreary academic lives.

Not that Sam was an expert. In fact, he was a royal screw-up when it came to sex, pardon the pun. He had a gorgeous, willing girlfriend, who, even though she was only a high school senior, was still so hot that his friends envied him. But she'd cheated on him. And he didn't have the guts to confront her about it. He wasn't even sure it was worth it, especially after what happened the other night. He'd gotten himself shitfaced and, pissed at Gaia, pissed at Heather, so freaking sick of school and studying and ice and snow—he'd done the dirty with a woman he'd met in a bar. They'd been chatting, friendly-like, and then she put her hand on his thigh and suddenly they were leaving the bar together.

Then there had been the soul-destroying event of

finding out that the woman was none other than Gaia's guardian, Ella Niven. Despite himself, Sam groaned out loud. When he'd found out, he'd almost thrown his guts up, all over Gaia's front door. Man, he was lower than low. Lower than a snake's belly. Lower than a—

This was so messed up. First off, he had to break it off with Heather soon. He was treating her like shit, even though he didn't mean to. She was treating him like shit, too.

If he didn't get the balls to break up with her, it would never happen. He wasn't blind. He knew it was a big prestige thing for her to have a college boyfriend. And she probably cared for him. If he didn't break up with her, they would just drift along in this lame-ass way, neither of them happy, until finally, *boom.* They'd be standing at the altar pledging to go through with this sham of a life forever. He couldn't let that happen. He was a man. A man had balls. He would find the balls to break up with Heather.

Mindlessly, Sam's gaze drifted down to the text page before him. It was almost a full-page, head-on view of A Male's Reproductive Organs. The Non-Excited State. Sam stared at it blankly. *Oh, right,* he thought bleakly. Balls.

A Sisterly Thing

HEATHER LOOKED AT THE SEE-through clear plastic princess phone on her bedside table. It was not ringing. It had not rung in much too long. *Maybe Sam has forgotten how to dial,* Heather thought sarcastically. *Maybe Sam has forgotten that phones exist. That bastard, maybe he's forgotten I exist.*

The phone sat there silently. *Okay, I'm a modern woman,* thought Heather. *I can express my needs. Right now I need a boyfriend who adores me. Right now I need to go to bed with Sam and have him hold me. Because when we're in bed, I can forget about everything else for a while. Forget about Gaia, forget about Ed, forget about my family.*

Heather picked up the receiver and punched in memory dial #1. On the other end, the phone in Sam's dorm suite rang and rang. "Pick it up," Heather said softly. "Pick it up, you jerk. Be there."

"Hello?"

Heather instantly assessed it as a non-Sam voice.

"This is Heather," she said.

"Heather, babe, it's Will."

"Hi, Will. Listen, is Sam there?"

"No dice," said Will. "Sam is wearing out the study chairs over at the library. His dad had his hide over Christmas because of his grades."

221

"Yeah, I know," said Heather. "So he's at the library?"

"Yep. I'll tell him you called, okay?"

"Okay." Heather hung up the phone. Being at the library, studying alone, was perhaps almost a partial excuse for not calling. And Heather did know that Sam's dad, the earnest Dr. Moon, had really gotten on Sam's case about his grades. So Sam was studying at the library. He wasn't somewhere with someone else. Like Gaia. As soon as the thought intruded, Heather quickly shut it out. God, if only Gaia would just get hit by a truck or something, Heather's life would be almost bearable again. For Heather, Gaia's existence was like getting clubbed in the head all the time and still trying to live a normal life.

Flopping over on her pillow, Heather tried to decide if she should go by the NYU library. Just pretend to be popping in. After all, her school had library privileges. She could say she needed to look something up. Then maybe she could convince Sam that he had studied enough, and they could go get coffee, and then they could swing by his dorm room . . . and then she would get home at two o'clock in the morning on a school night and Heather's parents would plotz.

Also, how likely was it that she would find him? How humiliating was it to plan a trip to the library on a Thursday night, hoping to run into a boyfriend who was treating you like shit? It was ridiculously humiliating, that's what. To hell with him. She would go out by herself, or with her sister Phoebe. Then when Sam called, *she* would be out. The ball would be in her court. And she wouldn't call him back for two frigging days, that jerk.

Heather scrambled off her bed. Maybe Phoebe would be into catching an early movie at the Angelika or something. A sisterly thing.

A bathroom connected Heather and Phoebe's bedrooms. When Heather heard the shower water shut off, she gave the door a brief tap and opened it.

"Hey, Feeb, I have a great idea," Heather began.

Phoebe had just stepped out of the shower and was reaching for a fluffy gold towel. It took only moments for Heather's gaze to sweep her sister's body. She blinked as Phoebe quickly wrapped herself in the towel, brushing long wet strands of hair out of the way.

"Whoa," Heather said without thinking. "You're . . . really skinny."

Really skinny didn't begin to describe what Heather had caught a glimpse of. She knew Phoebe had been dieting a lot—an attempt to get rid of the freshman fifteen she'd put on last year. But until now she'd simply thought Phoebe looked fabulous, model-slim in her bulky winter clothes. Naked, Phoebe looked like something else. Her elbows were whitened points. Her knees had sags around them, like an old lady's. Extra skin. Heather had been able to see Phoebe's rib bones through her skin, and her two hip bones jutted out like clothes hangers. She was much too thin.

Phoebe briskly started toweling her hair. "Thanks," she said casually.

"Like maybe you don't need to diet anymore," Heather said carefully. Now that she looked closely, she saw her sister's skin stretched taut over her facial bones. Her eyes looked deep-set, her cheekbones carved and prominent. Without makeup, her sister looked pale, anemic, underfed. With makeup, Heather knew, Phoebe looked stunning.

Bending over, Phoebe combed her hair out with her fingers, then expertly wrapped a towel around her head. She stood up and tucked in the towel ends. She smiled at Heather, and it suddenly seemed garish, skeletal. Heather began to feel as if she was about to freak out. "Heath-er," Phoebe said in an older-sister singsong. "I'm not dieting anymore. I'm just watching my weight. Trying not to go overboard. You won't believe how awful it was when I was practically a size nine! It was like, I couldn't button anything. I'm never going there again, let me tell you."

Phoebe brushed past Heather and went into her own room, but didn't start getting dressed. *She's waiting for me to leave,* Heather thought numbly.

"No kidding, Feeb," Heather said. "I mean, of course you don't want to be a size nine. But you don't want to be a size zero, either. I think you could lighten up, maybe even put on a few pounds."

"Oh, no way," said Phoebe, sounding irritated. "My body is finally the way I want it. No way am I going to sabotage it now." Her eyebrows came together and she looked at Heather with narrowed eyes. "You know, maybe you're just jealous."

Heather didn't know what to say. Her? Heather Gannis? Jealous? Not in a million years. She opened her mouth to say as much to Phoebe, but on second thought, closed it again without a word. Phoebe turned her back on Heather and opened her closet door. "Okay, clear out. I have to get dressed."

It was a dismissal, and Heather cleared out. There was no way she would go to a movie with Phoebe now. Instead, she went to find their mother.

"Mom?" Heather tapped on the door of her mother's bedroom. Mrs. Gannis was stretched out on her bed, reading a magazine.

"Yes?"

Heather took a deep breath. Her mother had never been easy to talk to. It was as if she had done her job by producing three children, and after that, they were kind of on their own. Maybe that wasn't fair. Heather knew it wasn't easy, living with Dad's reversal of fortune. Her mom had signed on for one kind of lifestyle, and now all of a sudden she was practically clipping coupons. But then, it was tough on all of them.

"Mom, have you noticed how Phoebe looks lately?" Feeling like a rat, Heather came in and perched on the end of her mother's bed. If Phoebe knew she was doing this, all hell would break loose.

Mrs. Gannis looked up, smiled. "Yes, she looks marvelous, doesn't she? I'm so proud of her. She looked simply awful when she got back from that college."

"Um, you don't think she looks a little . . . too thin?"

Her mother gave a short laugh. "Oh, you can never be too rich or too thin. Who said that?"

"I don't know," Heather said impatiently. "But you can be too thin, Mom. And Phoebe—you can see her bones. I think she's lost too much weight."

Sitting up, her mother managed to look both insufferably patient and a bit irritated. "Darling, she looks wonderful. There's nothing wrong with her. Heavens, when I was her age, I wore a size two. The women in our family are small-boned, that's all. Now don't worry about Phoebe. I don't want you telling her she's too thin. Next thing you know, she'll be putting on weight again, and we don't want that." She lay back and flipped a page in her magazine.

Dismissed again. Heather went back to her room, feeling more down than she had in oh, about two hours.

HOW can I express my feelings toward my only brother's only child? I can tell you that I hate my brother, but the word hate doesn't really begin to cover the depth of the feeling I have for him, my identical twin. He is light, I am darkness. He is a plodding government worker—I am exquisitely subtle in my occupation. I have raised what I do to the level of an art. He cannot approach my greatness. Every day that he lives, he taints my own existence. How can I achieve perfection if my identical twin is so flawed, so spineless, so completely lacking in nuance, in grace, in achievement? It is clear that my brother's days must be brought to an end soon. Only by standing alone can I attain my final destiny.

And then there's Gaia. My niece. Katia's child. The child that should have been mine, would have been mine—will someday be mine. Gaia is poised on the brink

of greatness. I can see that now.
Before, I thought she had potential. Now, seeing her reactions
to this latest test, the death of
the girl Mary, I am convinced
Gaia is almost ready to break
free from her restraining
chrysalis. She is showing
strength beyond measure. She is
unclouded by emotion. She is free
of sentimentality. She will come
to me soon.

DON'T MISS
FEARLESS #9
BLOOD
COMING NEXT MONTH
FROM POCKET PULSE

Gaia's Journal.

FEAR-1

Think you know Gaia?
Think again.

There's only one way to get the real 411 on this mysterious, butt-kicking New York City teen hero—and that's by logging on to **www.alloy.com**

What you'll find:

🌸 Poetry 🌸

Gaia's Poetry.

Hey, you can't be out knocking around the bad guys all day long...a girl's gotta spend a little time getting in touch with her inner spirit. Gaia writes poems about love, life, friends, growing up, her dad, her "family," and—oh yeah—saving the world. Read 'em at Alloy.com...and post your own poems, too.

C://GAIA

Gaia's Homepage.

Gaia's got her own homepage on the Internet, and it's full of all kinds of insider info you won't find in the book. But of course, not everyone can see it. (Gaia keeps this stuff on the down low.) But at Alloy.com, you'll get the password.